The Scourge Between Stars

The Scourge Between Stars

NESS BROWN

NIGHTFIRE

TOR PUBLISHING GROUP
NEW YORK

THE SCOURGE BETWEEN STARS

A Nightfire Book
Published by Tom Doherty Associates / Tor Publishing Group
120 Broadway
New York, NY 10271

www.tornightfire.com

Nightfire™ is a trademark of Macmillan Publishing Group, LLC.

The Library of Congress Cataloging-in-Publication Data
is available upon request.

ISBN 978-1-250-83468-3 (trade paperback)
ISBN 978-1-250-83469-0 (ebook)

Our books may be purchased in bulk for promotional, educational, or business use. Please contact your local bookseller or the Macmillan Corporate and Premium Sales Department at 1-800-221-7945, extension 5442, or by email at MacmillanSpecialMarkets@macmillan.com.

First Edition: 2023

Printed in the United States of America

0 9 8 7 6 5 4 3 2 1

TO MY PARENTS,
WHO GAVE ME THEIR LOVE FOR
ALL THINGS STRANGE,
SPOOKY, AND SPECULATIVE.

THANK YOU FOR SHARING YOUR
PASSIONS AND INDULGING MINE.
THIS ONE IS FOR YOU.

The Scourge Between Stars

The Sun was a golden stitch in the black tapestry of the void, just one needlepoint among thousands visible through the *Calypso*'s observation deck window. It made an extra zag in the sawtooth constellation of Cassiopeia, even though the ship had left Proxima b a century ago. The Sun should be blinding by now, the biggest thing in the sky, but Jacklyn still needed the ship's astronautical charts to tell which star it was. Which star was home.

The observation deck was dark. Infrared sensors could see her sitting against the deck's pressure glass, just a few inches from the vacuum of space, but she had been doing calculations in her head for long enough that motion detectors had forgotten her and reserve lighting had blinked off to conserve power. The math was bleak.

None of the ward representatives at today's briefing had liked her results either. Reclamation couldn't divert any more water to Orion Ward; Foodstuffs couldn't violate rations for Cygnus Ward. Jacklyn had crunched the numbers for them, but the reps still expected her to hand over resources the ship didn't have. Only a few of them had appreciated her invitation to go back to Proxima b and get more themselves.

Their forebears had taken only fifty years to sail from their burning home world to the false promise of a new start. At their current hamstrung pace, Jacklyn's crew would take centuries. They had two miserable choices: limp backward to surely meet death, or crawl forward and maybe prolong it.

Neither option had yet pulled ahead. Jacklyn wanted to ask for the consensus of the *Tiamat* or the *Pele,* but Comms hadn't made contact with the other ships in the Goddess Flotilla in months. They hadn't heard from the rest of the fleet in much longer. They would have to make their own graves.

Recycled air from the deck's vents blew across Jacklyn's nape, raising the wiry hairs there. The prickling sensation pulled her out of her thoughts and into the sudden clench of hyperawareness. She strained her ears, but the only sounds on the deck were the humming of the grav system and the metallic groaning of a tired spaceship a few decades away from decay. Right as she considered waving an arm to trigger the lights, a voice whispered in the darkness right next to her.

"Jack."

Jacklyn flinched, jerking her hands up. The motion made light flood the deck, blinding her.

Artificial breath puffed against her ear. "It's only me."

Jacklyn didn't relax. She blinked iridescent spots out of her eyes and gritted out, "I told you to quit sneaking up on me, damn it."

"I'm sorry." Watson's voice modulated regretfully. Its glowing blue eyes stared back at her without blinking where it crouched beside her.

Jacklyn suppressed a shudder and pushed her braids back with the beanie she had taken off to think. "What do you want?"

"The doctor asked for you." The android stood up in a well-oiled stretch of repurposed metal. "He's made progress."

A few objections leaped to the tip of Jacklyn's tongue. The first was for Watson to stop calling the man a doctor; he was the head technician of Data, not Sickbay. The other was for the head technician to remove Watson's new social behaviors; she hated the droid even more now that it could experiment with tone and body language.

"We had a briefing during alpha shift." She rocked onto her feet, dwarfing Watson by a whole head. "Why didn't he say anything then?"

Watson smiled stiffly. "He wants to show you."

Rolling her eyes, Jacklyn gathered her scuffed datapad and left the observation deck without waiting for Watson. A few swipes on the pad brought up a holographic schematic of the ship; all was well besides the red-flagged labs deck, still under repair. Jacklyn had been on that deck when the hull was breached—the memory of foul-smelling fire suppressant, shrieking repressurization alarms, and empty eyes staring into hers flashed through her mind. She pinched her arm for focus and stepped into the closest lift, where the droid caught up with her.

The ride up to the tactics deck was short but uncomfortable. By the time Jacklyn was ready to snap at Watson's mechanical attempts at small talk, the lift doors hissed open and admitted them to one of the long corridors that stretched between the hull of the *Calypso* and her keel like the spokes of a wheel.

They took a gangway all the way to the deck's central atrium, a space in the ship's ribcage where her blood and guts ran along the walls and floors in miles of wiring and piping. They walked the circumference until they hit the doors to Data, one of the most cramped parts of the ship.

The department was a honeycomb of blinking consoles and constant readouts, each techie's hexagon crowded with terminals. Wires stretched hazardously across aisles; extra screens hung precariously from jury-rigged mounts. Despite Ventilation's best efforts, even though every surface was practically oozing heat-sink paste, it was oppressively hot.

Jacklyn received harried salutes from the few personnel who glanced up as she climbed through the clutter to the head technician's office, a loft that hung over the rest of the hive. She barely finished waving them at ease before they went back to their analyses. She wasn't bothered—she wasn't the *Calypso*'s real captain anyway.

Otto Watson was inside his office, engrossed in the terminals taking up the entire wall, curled up like a bug in his chair. Jacklyn got a headache just looking at the monitors flashing raw input from around the ship, but he seemed to have no trouble parsing the data with his bare eyes.

"The droid said you have a progress report," Jacklyn said tersely.

Otto startled, kicking away from his console. "Jack! That was quick. Usually I have to wait a blue moon for a visit."

She didn't laugh. "What's so secretive that you couldn't tell everyone earlier?" They could have used some good news at the briefing, which was otherwise spent discussing how close the *Calypso* was to collapse.

Otto's eyes got feverishly bright. "Eureka."

Jacklyn had heard that before. "Explain."

Otto beckoned Watson over and pulled it close with an arm around its shoulders. The sight of Otto's space-pale hand against its artificial skin, the same color as Jacklyn's, rankled. That he had given it his own name rankled worse.

"Three months ago the third engineer sanctioned the diversion of extra power to Sensors," he said, hushed. "Ship receivers were tuned to maximum sensitivity for eight hours. We don't have any extra cache space here, so Watson is holding on to the data for now." He tapped Watson's temple with a bony knuckle, right beside the crack that split its faceplate from brow to chin.

Jacklyn was almost too irked by the touch to parse the implications. A second later she sucked in a breath. "You crammed all that information into the droid? Are you trying to fry its brains out of its skull?" She turned incredulously to Watson, whose synthetic expression was as placid as ever.

Otto's lips pursed at the interruption. "Watson is the most advanced post-zettascale system ever constructed." He didn't have the decency, as its creator, to blush as he said so. "It's about as difficult for her to ingest the data as it is for you and me to take a biscuit with our coffee."

Jacklyn hated when he gave the droid pronouns. "You took info that Sensors usually forwards to Comms and jammed it inside Watson," she summarized, enjoying Otto's scowl. "Why?"

"I'm doing much more than that," he insisted. "I've developed and imported into Watson a processing library more sophisticated than anything Data has ever run before. This morning I put the finishing touches on a new series of tasks that should be able to find what we've been missing."

Ever since the fleet decided to forsake the failed colony on Proxima b, they'd been creeping along at twenty-second-century speeds, feeling their way forward blindly. The prospect of finally being able to *see* was astonishing. For the first time since she was a girl, since the first time she felt the *Calypso* shudder and groan under the godly blow of an invisible, cosmic hand, Jacklyn allowed herself to wonder if they really could make it across the remaining trillions of kilometers of their journey alive.

Otto saw her seedling of hope and ran a proud, proprietary hand down Watson's back. The smile sprouting across Jacklyn's face withered.

"Have you tested the tasks?" Her voice came out hard.

"Just once," Otto admitted. "That's all I had time for after the briefing. That's why I had Watson escort you here."

He pushed Watson between them and curled his long fingers over its shoulders, leaning down by its ear to order, "Demonstrate."

Watson obeyed. The droid's jaw dropped in a too-wide yawn, hanging open like a hinge. Gooseflesh rose along Jacklyn's arms at the unnatural gape. She expected Watson to speak, but words were not what came out.

The sound it emitted from its gaping mouth began as static, a fuzzy hum that Jacklyn could've mistaken for raw noise: vibrations from the *Calypso*'s energy core, pulsar chatter, the constant background hum of the universe itself. Then the sound started to take shape.

The static warbled into long, distinct notes. It reminded Jacklyn of recordings she had heard of old sounds from Earth: plaintive humpback whale song, or the dissonance of a tuning orchestra. The notes started to pulse, each throb of noise wavering in pitch, almost like words in some celestial sentence.

Something about it made her gooseflesh turn into an outright chill. With astrophysical and instrumental sources ruled out, there were only a few things it could be.

"I can only speculate," Otto said, kneading Watson's unyielding shoulders excitedly. "But this might be the way forward."

Jacklyn fisted her hands in the fabric of her uniform, feeling some strange crossbreed of wonder and unease. "How long will it take to decipher?"

"It could take weeks—months—*years* to translate this data." Otto hummed. "Perhaps longer to figure out how to use it to map a safe route."

Jacklyn had never been planetside in her life. The first generation of settlers had left Earth over two hundred years ago, and the failed colonists had fled Proxima b in disgrace several decades before she was born. She had only ever known the *Calypso*'s artificial light and gravity, its recycled atmosphere and nutrients. The daydreams from her childhood—of real soil squishing between her toes, of ancient air circulating through her lungs—played in her mind again.

But in her dreams she had always emerged from the *Calypso* after her father and mother, with her sister beside her. No matter the promise this signal held, that dream would never come true. She was painfully reminded of that by the eerie sound floating out of Watson's familiar face, a face stolen from the grave.

She looked away. "Turn it off."

"I trust you understand the magnitude of this moment,"

Otto said, closing Watson's mouth and cutting off the transmission.

"Of course," Jacklyn gritted out, wanting to slap his hands away.

"We'll still be in danger until we're back on Earth," he warned, "but this signal might be our species's first lick of luck in centuries."

Jacklyn stared at Watson, who bore Otto's skinny hands on its artificial skin with fish-eyed patience. "Might." She scowled.

"Watson could be the key to saving humanity," Otto said, brushing back the droid's coily hair and cupping its cheek in his clammy palm.

Anger and nausea roiled in Jacklyn's gut. For the sake of the ship she had spent the last three months trying to swallow her disgust, her resentment, her grief. Now all of those threatened to rise in her gullet.

"Carry on then," she snapped. Otto jumped at her tone, but she wasn't looking at him—she was looking at Watson, who tilted its head at her curiously. Unable to stomach its docility anymore, she turned on her heel and stalked out of the office.

"I'll message you with any developments!" Otto called.

Jacklyn held her breath through Data's oppressive heat until she could make it back to the cool air of the atrium, where she was in no danger of vomiting all over the processors that could take them home.

※

Jacklyn exited the lift on the command quarters deck. She almost regretted storming out of Data, but just thinking about Otto going through the ship's salvaged metal and choosing a face for his pet droid that Jacklyn had known and loved made her stomach clench again. She pinched her arm as she stepped onto the gangway.

Her bootsteps echoed down the long corridor as she marched toward the bridge crew quarters. It was empty—everyone was already at their stations, spending their leisure time down in the wards, or sleeping off their last shift in their bunks. Nobody else visited the captain's bunk except her.

She halted in front of the door marked with the name ALBRIGHT. For a long time she stood there clenching and unclenching her hands, glad that no one could see her wrestle with the decision to knock. Just before the gangway lights blinked off, she banged a fist against the door.

There was, unsurprisingly, no answer.

Jacklyn let out a slow breath, waiting until her lungs burned before sucking in the next. "Captain," she called. She paused for an acknowledgment that didn't come. "I'm here to report ship and mission status."

She looked as stupid yelling outside the bulkhead now as she had the first twenty times. "We voted to decelerate again today. Repairs are ahead of schedule, but we can barely take another hit." She recited the items from the briefing at the wall. "I vetoed the delivery of extra resources to Orion and Cygnus Wards. There will be more demonstrations, but our ration levels are already critical." After a pause, she shared what had happened in Data. "Otto may have figured out a way to avoid the engagements."

That was their word for the sudden, catastrophic blows that struck the *Calypso* without warning. Sometimes months would pass between engagements, sometimes only days. There was no way to predict when and where the next hit would come; that was beyond the capabilities of their current systems.

At least three ships in the Goddess Flotilla—the *Ishtar,* the *Freya*, and the *Lieu Hanh*—had gone silent somewhere in the last few billion kilometers. Communications had degraded so badly that Jacklyn didn't even know if the Hero or Epic Flotillas were still flying. It was entirely possible that they had been swatted like bugs by the dangerous force lurking in the void.

If Otto was right, then Watson had just discovered their first confirmation of something else out there in the space between stars, perhaps the very thing that took the *Calypso* between its teeth at random and shook. Their systems hadn't been powerful enough to detect anything during engagements, until now. If they could finally sense them, they could survive them.

"That souped-up droid of his," Jacklyn continued. "He completely revamped its protocols—now it makes Comms look like a joke. It might even be able to keep us all alive."

No response.

Jacklyn cursed the part of herself that was still hurt by the silence. Her throat tightened, and her voice lowered until there was no way anyone would hear her through the door anyway.

"Dad," she choked out, leaning forward to let her forehead thunk against the metal. She wasn't sad, not anymore; the tears that stung the backs of her eyes were hot and angry. "How long are you going to make me do this by myself?"

The captain had stopped answering his comms and leaving his quarters last week. As the first mate, she could only cover for him for so long. She stared at the closed door, wondering for the nth time if she should rip out the panel next to it, scramble the wires controlling the mechanism, and force her way in.

The vomitous shock and horror she had felt five years ago, when she did the same to her mother's quarters, was still fresh. She worried that she'd find Captain Noah Albright just like she had found Tegan Albright: sprawled across the bunk floor, stiff and blood-swollen on one side, staring out way beyond the Sun with wide, filmy eyes.

That was absurd, since infrared sensors in the captain's bunk would've alerted her already. But it was a stain she couldn't wash from her mind.

She yanked off her beanie and slid down the wall until her head hung between her knees. Her braids fell forward in a curtain around her face. In that small privacy she let herself cry. Her shoulders shook quietly for several minutes; she had dammed up so much over the last three months.

When she was done, she wiped her uniform sleeve across her face and gathered her braids back to order. She turned sharply from the captain's bunk. There was no more time to waste waiting for relief that wouldn't come, not when the next threat to their survival surely would.

✳

Jacklyn completed her rounds right before the start of the next gamma shift. After alpha shift she had relinquished the conn to the second mate and taken a lift downship to perform the off-duty routine she had carried out ever since becoming first mate: clear each deck and confirm for herself that the *Calypso* was still mostly spaceworthy.

The five wards comprised thirty decks of galleys and messes, gymnasiums and recreation rooms, libraries and schools, religious alcoves and nurseries, as well as quarters for the rest of the six-thousand-member crew. Jacklyn patrolled each one, marking down the repair teams hustling to reconstruction sites, the cargo droids pushing supply carts, the off-duty staff sipping moonshine. All the while she ignored the bitter looks from the huddles of crew members that had begun gathering lately in dark corners of the ship.

The doors to the silos were secure. The conditions in the farms read Earth-normal. Sickbay had finally discharged all but a fragile few patients. Security had nothing to report. In record time Jacklyn landed all the way down in Engineering, where she found the second engineer scrolling through projections of the *Calypso*'s propulsion module on a holographic table. He didn't look happy.

She knocked on the doorframe. "Problem, Kachi?"

The storm clouds on Onyekachi James's face lightened. "Hey, Jack. Same shit, different day."

"Shock absorbers?" she asked sympathetically.

"Shock absorbers," he sighed. "I get the backlash about decelerating, but it's the only reason we're not meat splatter on the walls. Everything from the pusher plate to the meteoroid shield is screwed up. If we tried going at pre-Proxima speeds, we'd get juiced by all the g's."

He'd explained it to her before—the decades that the fleet

had spent on Proxima b, exposed even at the terminator to the host star's radiation tantrums, had corroded a number of systems and machines.

"The engagements don't help," he said bitterly.

When the engagements first started, the engineers had hypothesized that the fleet had encountered some kind of interstellar energy fluid, though their forebears hadn't reported anything of the kind. As the engagements got worse, conservative explanations were replaced with the harrowing realization that they might not be the only ones roaming the void.

Jacklyn's mother used to call the engagements *the gods duking it out.*

The ones behind the engagements probably weren't gods, even with the ability to make interstellar war, but they were definitely too advanced for the fleet's antiquated systems to detect or hail. The *Calypso* had no way of sidestepping the invisible crossfire of the skirmish that had drifted into their neighborhood since their species had last crossed this empty space.

Jacklyn wished she had good news for Onyekachi, but it was in short supply. She would have to wait until Watson gave them more than whale song for that. Until the droid found a way off the board of whatever dangerous game into which the fleet had unwittingly wandered, or even a way to communicate with the players.

"Keep up the good work," Jacklyn said.

Onyekachi shot finger guns at her on her way back to the lift.

Jacklyn recognized the compulsiveness in the decision to

make one last trip to the bridge, but she indulged herself anyway. The second mate, Asher Kind, still had the conn; he rolled his eyes as soon as she stepped through the doors.

"Go to bed," he said in lieu of a greeting.

"This is my last stop," Jacklyn promised.

Asher huffed. "You and Jolie deserve each other."

Flustered, Jacklyn scanned the room; from the captain's vantage point she could see every station, several holo-schematics displaying the *Calypso*'s vitals, and the entire viewfinder looking out into the blackness of space. It was too bright to see the tapestry of constellations, but this screen wasn't for stargazing—it was overlaid with coordinates and trajectories.

Jacklyn wasn't surprised to see the third mate, Jolie Singh, at the sensors console, keeping a keen eye on the deflector shield preventing the ship from getting turned into scrap by stray particles; she always reported to the bridge a few minutes ahead of her command. Feeling Jacklyn's attention on the waterfall of her glossy hair, Jolie glanced up and met her eyes with unerring accuracy. She examined the shy look on Jacklyn's face and then smirked.

Cheeks hot, Jacklyn quickly looked away. "Any updates?"

Asher was smug. "None. Just another few trillion kilometers of nothing ahead."

"Or worse," Jacklyn murmured to herself.

Right as the words left her lips, the bridge erupted with blaring, staticky noise.

Every head snapped toward the communications station. The console was crackling with sound, gone unexpectedly live. The head comms techie's fingers raced across the switchboard, trying to shut off the harsh hissing.

"Comms?" Asher asked sharply.

The techie frowned at his station and reported, "Malfunction."

Jacklyn waited for him to wrestle the console back under control, but the speakers continued spitting and popping. "What is that?" she finally asked.

For the first time since he joined the bridge crew, the techie hesitated. "A message."

Jacklyn was at the comms station before she thought to move, nearly checking Asher with her shoulder as they both came over to listen.

The signal-to-noise ratio was abysmally low. This was nothing like the scrubbed-up audio she had heard in Data. Punches in the static vaguely reminded her of words, but she couldn't make out anything coherent. Just as she leaned closer to the garbled sound, the transmission cut out.

"Were you recording?" Asher demanded.

He accepted the techie's withering look. "Stand by."

Asher turned to the rest of the bridge. "Back to stations." The ship trembled a little underfoot as the helmsman returned it dutifully to course.

Jacklyn waited impatiently while the techie doctored the damaged broadcast with one hand and crammed his earpiece in with the other so hard she worried he might rupture something. His face went tight as he listened to the replay.

"Jack, Asher," he said lowly. Jacklyn had never heard him sound unsettled before. "Listen."

She took the offered earpiece.

The static buzzed in her ear again, but this time it fizzled into clarity. The last fragment of the message came out loud and clear.

"... is ... the *Atalanta*. Something—ssssss—ollow ... xima. It's ... the ship. Wa—ssssss—epeat, warning ... ssssss—ssssss—ssssss ... on't ... epeat, don't ... ssssss. This is Captain Isidora of the *Atalanta*. I—ssssss—anyone listening. Please. Don't open the door."

2

The labs deck was eerily empty without the familiar swarm of researchers scuttling around. Instead of distracted techies and diligent work droids, there were warning holograms and scaffolding skeletons. The only other people on the deck were engineers completing repairs to the hole busted in the *Calypso*'s hull. Now that they had finished going through debris and jettisoning what couldn't be recycled, rebuilding had begun in earnest.

Jacklyn should've been in her bunk, but she had gasped awake from yet another nightmare earlier: air pipes leaking precious oxygen in stinging bursts, walls turning into floors as onboard gravity malfunctioned, blood gurgling from a throat constricting around her name. There was no falling back to sleep after that.

And there was the niggling mystery of the *Atalanta*'s transmission. She had wasted an hour on her cot trying to imagine the context of the message. Neither Asher nor Jolie could suggest any useful interpretations when they had retreated to the captain's ready room to discuss. There were several obvious doors not to open on a spaceship, but which one could warrant a message like that?

Jacklyn came to the labs deck to assist where she could. At first Viktorija Novak had protested her presence. Despite being one of the few crew members bigger than Jacklyn, the first engineer was too nice to tell her to get lost. Jacklyn exploited that weakness until Viktorija pointed her in the direction of a low-priority task where she wouldn't be in the way.

She was fixing a pressure-dented maintenance hatch in the gangway, far from the delicate work around the hull breach. If she stood in the deck's atrium, she could probably hear the ruckus of the construction. All the way over by the astrophysics lab, however, it was silent except for the metallic sounds of the *Calypso*'s indigestion.

The droid helping her was a hypodroid, a class below the palindroids that assisted the lab techies and much less sophisticated than an android like Watson. Its face was a featureless plate, and its speech capabilities were rudimentary. Somehow that had become weird to Jacklyn. The droid held the hatch open for her while she made sure its seal was still airtight.

She kicked the hatch back to something like smoothness, swinging her legs out of the way as the droid let it drop with a heavy thud. It motored over to a wall panel to tick the task off the communal repairs checklist. She expected it to move on to the next job, but it turned back to her.

"Anomaly detected," it announced.

Jacklyn frowned down at their handiwork. "In the hatch?"

"Negative," the droid said. "In the wall."

Jacklyn scanned the sides of the corridor as far as she could see; none of the bulkheads were so much as scratched. "What kind of anomaly?"

The droid whirred in consideration. Jacklyn's foot tapped in annoyance. "Hey," she said after a minute. "What kind of—"

A bang reverberated down the gangway.

Jacklyn startled, whipping her head around. The corridor was still empty; the echo of the sound wavered and then disappeared around the passage's distant end.

"What was that?" she asked the droid. It could have been a panel falling from the ceiling or one of the repair crew clanking over this way, but she couldn't see anything down the dark hall.

The droid didn't respond. Jacklyn bent to check its faceplate and was surprised to find that it had stalled, hot to the touch. She got ready to pull its plate and let the freezing corridor air equilibrate the excess heat, reaching for the too-warm metal.

Another bang shattered the quiet right next to her.

She flinched away from the droid, spinning around. They were still alone in the corridor. She didn't see anything on the deckhead or the gangway that could have made a noise like that. The only thing in front of her was the bulkhead.

"Anomaly in the wall . . . ?" she murmured. Maybe there was a busted pipe bucking against its fastenings, or a piece of debris rattling around behind the metal panels. She stepped forward to put her ear to the nearest one.

For several moments she heard nothing besides the *Calypso*'s inner workings. The sound had comforted her as a child, something else to listen to besides her parents' furious whispered arguments. At the very edge of her hearing, she noticed something underneath the hum of the grav and reclamation systems: a scratching noise, the kind of tinny shriek she used to make by dragging her nails down the wall of her bunk as a troubled kid. The moment she wondered what it could be, another bang thundered right under her cheek, nearly tossing her back on her ass.

She sucked in a breath. "Goddamn it."

The bang came again. And then again. Jacklyn's stomach knotted. What was this? A bubble in the intestines of the *Calypso*? In between the shuddering knocks on the bulkhead, the scratching came longer and louder.

Jacklyn jumped when the droid suddenly spoke.

"Anomaly detected," it droned. Its faceplate began to smoke. "Anomaly detected. Anomaly. Anomaly—"

Another bang, this one hard enough to shake the metal panel in front of her. Jacklyn's heart leaped into her throat; she took an involuntary step backward. Just as she turned to go find a maintenance techie, she slammed into something big and solid and went sprawling.

A shadow hunched over her, seizing her arm. Jacklyn's pulse spiked hard—she tried to thrash out of the tight grip, until she realized her overreaction. Standing above her was Viktorija.

"A little jumpy, Jack?" she quipped, hauling Jacklyn up with one hand and dusting off her uniform. She gave her a once-over and frowned when she noticed Jacklyn's wide eyes. "What's wrong?"

"Droid said there's an anomaly in the walls," she said. "Something's knocking around in there." She cocked one ear down the corridor, but all the clanging from before had ceased. Her heart rate slowed back to normal.

Viktorija dragged a hand down her face. "I'll have another droid look at the problem, since that one seems to have given up." She glanced over Jacklyn's shoulder at the smoking droid.

Jacklyn frowned. "Do the hypodroids often overheat like that?" She tallied up the number of them on the ship, estimating how long it would take to examine each unit for faulty cooling systems.

"Not at all," Viktorija said thoughtfully. "I'll take that one for inspection. Did Vidal come this way?"

"Huh?" Jacklyn was still smoothing down her braids and trying to do the math. She vaguely recognized the name.

"The mechanic with the Cygnus Ward tat on his neck," Viktorija described, indicating his height with her hand. According to the gesture he came up impressively to her chin. "He said he was going to get more epoxy from the machine shops, but he never came back."

Jacklyn hadn't seen anyone else in the corridor for more than an hour. "It was just me in here."

Viktorija scrutinized her. "Are you sure you're alright?" With her arms crossed she looked a few seconds away from ordering Jacklyn back to her quarters.

Jacklyn didn't need telling off; even she could tell it was time to get some rest. "Guess I am a little jumpy."

Both of them startled at the chime of her datapad in the quiet corridor. She fished it out of her pocket and opened the emergency message from the chief security officer blinking on the screen.

"Shit," Jacklyn hissed, pocketing the pad again. "I've got to go."

"What's wrong?" Viktorija asked, already calling the lift for her.

Jacklyn sighed. "There's a riot down in the wards."

❋

Homunculus Hall, the biggest mess in Carina Ward, was in tumult. The riot spanned the entire room—Jacklyn could see the different colored uniforms of Carina and Orion crew in the brawl, straining against the security officers pulling them apart. Within a disaster radius of overturned tables and wasted food, the rioters were throwing fists and—judging by the few people bleeding on the ground—worse. This was the ugliest so far of the demonstrations that had been picking up momentum for over a year now.

Jacklyn found Michiko Tomimori struggling at the edge of the crowd, trying with her officers to deescalate. Even though she only came up to Jacklyn's shoulders, the *Calypso*'s longest-standing security chief exuded a quiet menace that usually kept people in line. This was the first time her presence alone had failed to nip a confrontation in the bud. Jacklyn pulled her shoulders back as she rushed in to help.

"What's the situation?" She elbowed two crew members apart, blocking a wild swing from a rage-blind rioter.

"Jack." Michiko jerked someone else's wrist behind their back. "Galley staff called us in. Figured you'd still be awake." She knew Jacklyn well, even though it had been years since she used to come to Michiko's office after lessons and help watch live feeds of the ship's nooks and crannies.

The security line finally encircled the squabble, and, slowly, the mess began to simmer down. Medics rushed in to retrieve the injured. An officer bustled the dissident in Michiko's grip away. Jacklyn stood between the separated crew members like a warning, ignoring the rude shouts and fingers tossed her way by those who didn't appreciate the first mate's intervention.

"You should show your face to the reps," Michiko advised. "Get on good terms, or we'll have more demonstrations."

"Yes, sir." Jacklyn squeezed her way over to where the

reps from Carina and Orion were trying to calm their constituents while the ship's quartermaster, Panio Nizzola, told everybody off.

"It takes a lot of balls to harass Foodstuffs for doing their jobs," he shouted. "We're all hungry here! Rations and Reclamation are the only reasons we aren't all skeletons in our bunks."

Jacklyn ducked between the reps. "Everything alright here?" she half shouted over the noise.

"Just a little disagreement," Carina's rep yelled back, snapping his fingers warningly at the disgruntled crew behind him. He walked off without another word, but that was the first civil thing he had said to her in months—she took it as a victory.

"Thanks for coming down, Jack." Orion's rep gave her a thumbs-up, a rare friendly gesture. "But we've got this."

"I'll take a report of the incident," Jacklyn sighed. So much for good terms—but she supposed this was a step up from the hostile yelling at the last briefing.

She turned away from the reps herding their people to the lifts, and went to a fuming Panio in the middle of directing sanitation droids toward the petty destruction strewn across the mess. He saw her coming; she tilted her head discreetly and he peeled away to follow her into the galley, where there was ironic privacy in the bustling kitchen that hadn't stopped cooking despite the uproar.

"Hey," she said. "Tough palates out there?"

Panio stomped his foot. "If they don't like the food on-ship, they can try foraging outside."

She cracked a smile before leaning in close. "Your analysis?"

"Same thing I told the captain." Panio shrugged, still

flushed. "The farm techies are seeing what the poor bastards back on Earth saw. Our soil's exhausted."

Asher had mentioned this two weeks ago, right around the time he, Jacklyn, and Jolie started covering for her father's unusual absentmindedness. She wondered if this was why she caught Noah looking at silo stats the day before he disappeared. "How screwed are we?"

"Right now? Middling to fair," Panio admitted. "We'll need to open the stores."

The math came quickly to Jacklyn. Barely a fifth of the way back to their ancestral home, they were already going to dip into their reserves. It was a harder pill to swallow than the gruel she had to eat with the rest of the crew.

"Understood," she sighed. "Send me the numbers. I'll bring it up next briefing."

"Good luck," Panio said, running a hand down his face.

Jacklyn went back out into the mess. Michiko met her gaze as she followed her officers down to the security deck and told her very firmly with just her eyes to go straight to her bunk. Jacklyn, sideswiped by the exhaustion that had eluded her before, called the next lift to obey.

She almost wished she could sleep in Michiko's office again, in the place where she had learned to count instead of yell when things got overwhelming. But those days of letting someone else make the decisions and give the advice were done. She just needed enough sleep to get up and do it again tomorrow.

※

After her next shift, Jacklyn took a lift all the way down to Sickbay, dead on her feet. What little sleep she had gotten was disturbed by dreams about the gargled warning from the *Atalanta,* about doors that should stay shut. She came to pick up the prescription that muted her nightmares, but the chief medical officer intercepted her at the door.

"The captain," Wang Hsu said simply.

Jacklyn had nowhere near the energy for this conversation, but Wang admittedly looked worse. The CMO still had patients from the last engagement showing little sign of improvement, even after several stints in the surgery theater, and now some patients from the riot. He must be pulling double shifts.

She responded truthfully, "I have no idea."

Wang sucked in a breath. "Not even you?"

"No response," she said tightly.

He was quiet for a while. "Gamma shift," he said finally, in a tone that brooked no argument. "We're breaking in. We need Noah right now."

Jacklyn swallowed the denial that pushed up her gullet, a nausea born from nightmares of forcing open the captain's quarters and letting out a flood of blood into the corridor. The newly occupied cots in the med wing proved Wang's point. She couldn't indulge herself or her father anymore. "Fine. Gamma shift."

She left Wang to the people stretched out in the sickbeds, walking farther back. She bypassed the rehabilitation tanks, which she had only been inside twice: once as a girl, stricken by space sickness, and three months ago, restrained and sedated from a screaming fit. Those memories were still dark and broken, partly from the drugs and partly from the worst heartbreak she had ever felt in her life.

She stopped at the dispensary to pick up a refill of the

medication she had taken ever since. It managed the mood swings, loss of appetite, and periodic listlessness. The captain was prescribed something similar, though she had no idea if he was taking them. She would find out during gamma shift, she supposed. The prospect of seeing him face-to-face and demanding answers should have made her feel energized or even anxious. She mostly wanted to sleep.

She tossed her meds back with a drink offered by one of the nurse droids. Then she steeled herself and made her way down to Engineering, where she knew Otto and Watson would be for the droid's maintenance appointment.

She found them at a droid station, as well as a few assistants. Watson was being crowded where it lay on a worktable by Otto, the third engineer, and the head droid techie.

The way they loomed over the petite droid, poking and prodding at its gaping compartments, was disconcerting. For once the expression on Watson's faceplate wasn't neutral pleasantness; instead, its brows were pulled down over its glowing eyes. It was Jacklyn's first time seeing the droid fazed; her steps faltered on the way over.

They had opened its chassis to reapply pastes and check superconductor components in its processing equipment, which had probably processed more data in the last day than the *Calypso* had in the last six months. Even from afar Jacklyn noticed the corrosion next to what would have been its heart if it were human, and she could hear the techie explaining that the power draw of Watson's new caliber of calculations was overloading it.

The third engineer offered, "We prevent the *Calypso*'s overload with alternating metal lattices. I can make a mini lattice from our spare materials, but only one."

"Understood," Otto said, staring greedily down at Watson's bared innards. "Can we make the improvements now?"

"Give me three hours," the techie judged. "We should have everything replaced by then."

"Make it four," the third engineer said, helping the techie close Watson's chest and carry it away to the machine shop. "We gotta give Watson the lady treatment, after all."

Jacklyn's lip curled as they disappeared around the corner with the droid slung between them, leaving her and Otto alone. She watched them until they were out of sight, eyes on Watson's despondent face.

"Jack," Otto greeted her. He was also staring after Watson. "How kind of you to find me on your own."

She ignored that. "Have you cleaned all of the observation data?"

Otto nodded. "Most of it sounds like what you heard. The process gave Watson a bit of heartburn. Perhaps I was wrong about the biscuit."

Jacklyn didn't think he should be so blasé about Watson blowing out half its chest. "Have you tried the tasks?"

"Not yet," Otto admitted, rubbing the stubble on his neglected jaw. "I need a control dataset first, once Watson is cleaned up." He looked at Jacklyn appraisingly.

"What?" she asked, feeling cagey.

"I'd like you to keep Watson on the bridge for a shift," he requested. "Comms could give her a snack."

Jacklyn didn't like that idea at all. There were plenty of hypodroids who already fulfilled designated roles on the bridge. They didn't need an experimental android with untested processing up there as well.

Otto sensed her hesitance. "If we want to get back to Sol

in one piece, I need to debug her protocols. After that, we can finally perceive—perhaps even parley with—whoever else is out there. We'll never suffer another engagement again."

Jacklyn massaged her temples. "One hour on the bridge next alpha shift. That's it."

Otto smiled. It didn't put her much at ease. "Thank you, Jack. You and Watson are going to get us home."

✳

Jacklyn passed the time until gamma shift on the observation deck, staring at the Sun. It might be a little brighter than before—probably her own wishful thinking. They still had a long way to go before home loomed big and blue in the window.

Her father used to wax poetic about what it would feel like to touch the solid, fertile ground that had given birth to their species. As Jacklyn aged out of that optimism, she would remind him that both Earth and Proxima b had promised paradise before. He had been deep in thought recently, before he shut himself in—she wondered if his hope too had finally petered out. She could ask him after the shift change, right after she eviscerated him for neglecting his crew.

A noise ripped Jacklyn from her musings. She froze where she leaned against the pressure glass, holding her breath to listen. The deck was utterly silent, completely dark without reserve lighting since the motion detectors had forgotten her. She thought for a second that she had imagined the sound, until it came again.

She recognized it immediately: a bang in the bulkhead.

Viktorija hadn't sent any update on yesterday's mysterious noises beyond mentioning that Vidal still hadn't reported back. Jacklyn tried to remember if the pipes from the labs ran this way, if whatever had been rattling around below had been forced upward by ventilation currents or the ship's heat transfer system. She stepped forward to investigate.

Right away the hairs on her arms stood up. Even though she had moved from the window, the reserve lighting didn't turn on.

She sat here in the dark often, but moving through the shadowy deck was a different matter. She felt her way around the stargazing benches and came to a stop before the closest bulkhead. The silent, unlit deck was eerie enough that Jacklyn felt a little nervous, and foolish for it. She reached a hand out to the wall, shaking off the gooseflesh trying to rise under her uniform.

As soon as her fingers touched the metal panel, a bang like a gunshot cracked under her touch, making her spring back.

It came again, even louder. This time it was accompanied by a harsh, metallic scraping.

She stared at the horrible noise, like nails scoring the wall from the inside. Pressure-burst metal grinding shrilly against the interior structure? Jettisoned debris accidentally piped through the wrong system? Jacklyn cycled through possible explanations even as she shuddered, more and more unnerved with each deafening bang.

Something seized her arm.

A burst of adrenaline had Jacklyn lashing out instinctually. Her fist glanced off of metal—she hissed, snatching it back to cradle her knuckles.

"Jack."

Watson released its tight grip on her.

Jacklyn's unease curdled into anger at the sight of the droid. She stuck a smarting finger in the droid's face. "I *told* you—"

She forgot the rest when she noticed its eyes were shining the wrong color.

"Watson . . . ?" she asked lowly. The sickly yellow glow in Watson's face cast a jaundiced light between them, making the droid look wan and sick.

It had the same uncomfortable expression from before. The distress pulling at that familiar face made Jacklyn's heart skip a painful beat.

"They're opening the door," Watson whispered.

Jacklyn's stomach fell all the way to her boots. Before she could ask what the hell Watson meant, a boom shook the entire ship.

3

The *Calypso* rocked, tossing from side to side like a real ship on a sea. Jacklyn hit the deck window hard, cracking her head against the glass. Dazed and winded, she managed to flip at the last moment to avoid being crushed by Watson's immense weight as it fell after her. She worried about the sound the window made under the droid's dense limbs.

The grav system took several seconds to reset and drop them back down to the floor. Jacklyn's breathing and heart rate spiked as she flashed back to the last engagement, when she had watched her sister's body slam into the labs deck walls. She didn't even have the opportunity to pinch the memories away—the ship shuddered again, threatening to send her back on her ass.

She slapped her boots, turning on the magnetic soles. They suctioned her to the metal floor so she could finally get her feet under her. The moment she could stand upright, she ran for the lift, Watson keeping pace at her heels.

"What did you say?" she panted, skidding into the cab and jamming the lift buttons. It sped them upward to the topmost deck.

"They're opening the door," Watson repeated, still blinking at her with that sallow stare. It looked even more disturbing in the lift's emergency lights.

Jacklyn had questions—*who are they, which door*—but

there was no time to ask. When the lift opened, she burst into the controlled chaos of the bridge.

Jolie was sitting rigid in the captain's chair, giving terse orders to Sensors and Navigation. The viewfinder was epileptic with red warnings and blinking advisories; the ship schematic in the corner flashed a dozen new damage alerts.

"Divert power to Sensors," Jolie commanded. "Reduce velocity and cut the impulse engine. Proceed immediately on thrusters."

She stood up when she saw Jacklyn, filling her in before she could say *status report*. "We've been hit. Preliminary scans show that some of Perseus Ward has been sheared off."

Jacklyn missed her footing as she reeled. Necessity made her grit her teeth and pull herself together in the next step. "Navigation."

The nav techie's hands flew across her console, flagging the coordinates where they had suffered the engagement's first blow. "Computer's extrapolating a map now."

On the viewfinder several trajectories popped up. In between the lanes were starbursts representing where the next blows would likely come. Nav and Data had been working on these plots for decades, using past engagements to guess in real time the way through the minefields. Jacklyn looked back and forth between the possibilities, trying to make a split-second decision.

"Jolie," she murmured, "stats for option eta?" These trajectories were only suggestions; there was no guarantee that any of the options would deliver them to safety.

Jolie checked the nav display, tapping her datapad so hard it turned her brown knuckles white. "Sixty-five percent."

"Eta course, now," Jacklyn barked. Her father had taught

her to take anything better than fifty, since those odds didn't come along often. The ship lurched onto that trajectory.

On the other side of the bridge, the Sensors officer warned, "Jack, we're hemorrhaging. Ward decks."

On screen the ship's gas levels started to drop: percentages of nitrogen, oxygen, even the methane traces circulated by the farms all dwindled. If they didn't act fast, the numbers would plummet below what could be replaced by emergency reserves. Everyone onboard who couldn't reach their spacesuit in time would asphyxiate, and those who did would only have a few hours of air before they followed.

Jacklyn closed her eyes, weighing the consequences of what she had to do. She yearned for her father to walk through the lift doors right now. He was used to making these calls; he would know the right choice. He didn't show up, of course, even though the ship's klaxons were blaring at ear-splitting volume. The decision was on her.

"Seal the breach."

The bridge went silent; the only sounds were the muffled alarms from the other decks and the beeping of the ship's vitals on the viewfinder. The Sensors officer swallowed and obeyed. As soon as they input the commands for all corridors and vents around the leakage to snap shut, regardless of those on the other side, the hemorrhaging stopped and the levels flattened out.

Space was silent, but that didn't stop Jacklyn from hearing screams. She counted out ninety seconds in the remorseful quiet of the bridge before asking, "How is she?"

"Pulling against me," the helmsman reported. "She's hurt bad."

Jacklyn silently estimated the damages. Nearly every engagement had a body count, but this one would be worse.

"Jack!" The Comms officer made a strange noise. "We're picking up something."

Jacklyn practically teleported to their station. They had tried detecting signals in the middle of engagements before, but up until Otto's recent breakthrough they had recorded only space noise, their primitive equipment too far behind the apparent galactic standard to help.

Jacklyn could hear her own nervous pulse. "What is it?"

Before Comms could answer, Watson opened its mouth.

It had been standing silently in the bridge wing; Jacklyn had forgotten it was there. Staticky noise, not quite the sound that Jacklyn had heard in Data, came out of its yawning throat: an unsettling hiss that popped and crackled with the fuzziness of a lost signal. Someone else on the bridge gasped. Nearly everyone turned from their stations to look at Watson's unhinged jaw, the open maw vomiting that horrible sound.

"Watson," Jacklyn hissed. She couldn't have this kind of scene on the bridge right now.

The sound clicked off as Watson closed its mouth. A second later it announced, "It's coming through."

"What?" Jacklyn demanded, taking a step toward the droid before stopping in her tracks.

Oil seeped from Watson's face, from the crack along its temple and the false lids of its eyes. It ran clear at first, almost like tears, before it darkened and turned the shade of old, dried blood.

"It's coming through the door," it cried. "We have to close it. Close it—!"

Watson lunged for the comms station. Jacklyn dashed forward to catch it, but she was too slow. The Comms officer flinched out of the way, allowing Watson to reach out and drop a heavy hand on the console. The switchboard crunched under the weight of the dense metal. The circuitry whined for a moment, shedding sparks underneath Watson's palm.

Then the whole thing exploded.

A huge tongue of flame licked up the bulkhead from the console, sending up a chorus of cries. The closest officers were blasted back. Smoke flooded the bridge, followed immediately by the shrill screaming of a fire alarm. Emergency droids detached from the walls and motored over, smothering the fire with foamy suppressant.

It took only seconds to contain the blaze, but the damage had been done. The console was ruined, and its officer was rolling on the ground, clutching their face and shouting. Jacklyn caught a glimpse of blistered and raw skin all down their front before a palindroid shoved the hypodroids aside and picked the officer up. It rushed them to the lift, activating the button to drop straight down to Sickbay.

Jacklyn slid across the floor to the nav station, where Jolie and the nav techie were sprawled as well, knocked over by the blast. She stamped on the smolder eating away at the techie's uniform and jerked her up. "Can you stand?"

She shook the daze out of her eyes. "Yes, Jack."

"Get a diagnostic on Nav." Jacklyn needed to know how badly they had just been screwed.

"Aye, aye." The techie stumbled back to duty.

Jacklyn knelt beside Jolie, who was in much worse shape. It looked like she had smothered part of the blast with her body, taking the brunt of it for the crew behind her. The burns along her arms, face, and neck started to bubble. Jacklyn snatched an emergency medkit from the wall and upended its medigel on the seared pink skin, pulling Jolie's long hair back.

"Hey, look at me. Are you okay?" she asked loudly. "Jolie?"

Jolie squinted as if trying to read her lips and eventually just shook her head. Her pupils were different sizes, and her attention flitted from side to side, like she was chasing images.

Jacklyn pointed at another palindroid. "Take her to Sickbay now."

The droid carried Jolie to the next lift. Jacklyn looked after her until the doors closed.

Her dread prickled into something dark and bitter. Jacklyn crossed the bridge to where Watson was also sprawled on the floor, tossed several feet by the explosion. She hauled the android up in a fit of righteous strength, feeling no empathy at all for the metal bones showing through the melted false skin on its arms. She couldn't even muster the words she wanted to shout at it. Instead she dragged the droid to the other lift and threw it inside, smashing the button for the tactics deck. She would deal with that problem when they weren't sitting ducks.

The doors closed on Watson's twisted face, shiny with its peculiar tears. Jacklyn turned her back on it.

"Report!" she barked.

Sensors announced malfunctions spreading from the comms system—she told them to abort what they could and get the head systems techie to quarantine the problem. Corresponding nav functions were compromised, the helm seizing as a programmed precaution to too many sensor nodes going offline.

"I can't override them," the helmsman said apologetically.

Jacklyn slammed a hand down on the captain's chair in frustration. "What about my code?" She was second-in-command; her authorization had to count for something.

The nav techie shook her head. "We need the captain's."

Jacklyn nearly pulled out a few braids. "I'll see what I can do."

Asher was already stepping onto the bridge when she spun around. He took in the damage reports and Jacklyn's quick update with exhausted eyes and a clenched jaw. "You're trying the captain again?"

Jacklyn felt the same skepticism she heard in his voice. "I was going to break in with Wang right about now anyway."

"I'll take us through the engagement," he said before she could ask. "Good luck."

The rest of the bridge accepted the change of command without a hitch, but Jacklyn knew they were wondering now more than ever where the captain was, where he had been for the past week.

She went down to see for herself.

During the ride to the captain's quarters some of her adrenaline faded, but the anger zinging through her veins was just as galvanizing. She stormed up to her father's bunk and banged on the door so hard it hurt.

"Where the hell are you?" she yelled. "Don't you feel the shit going down right now? Don't you hear the goddamn alarms?"

She had been inside the captain's quarters countless times before. She knew there was a screen and terminal in there that provided ship updates at all hours. Its bell should have summoned him to the bridge after the first shake of the ship.

"Comms are completely dead. Sensors are compromised and the helm isn't responding. We're dead in the water. You have to give us the override before this engagement blows us to pieces."

She knew it was coming, but she was still enraged when she got only silence back. She scrabbled at the panel on the bulkhead until a fingernail broke, but it wouldn't unlock without the CMO's code and she didn't have the tools to pry up the interface.

"Are you really going to let us all die?" she seethed.

She kicked the door several times, hard enough to feel the blows through her reinforced boots. If he was sleeping, it would wake him. If he was awake and listening, it should mock him.

Still, there was only silence.

Jacklyn drew in a huge breath and screamed at the door. She screamed as loud as she could for as long as she could, voice ringing down the empty, dark, shuddering corridor. When her lungs started burning, she snapped her teeth down on the sound before turning on her heel and going back to where she was needed.

✳

The last time Jacklyn had worn her parade uniform was three months ago. She had been medicated at the time, both for her broken arm and for the hysteria she had been slipping in and out of since the eulogies for those lost in that attack. The captain and mates all wore their parade uniforms for the ship-wide announcements about the *Calypso*'s post-engagement status. Jacklyn's was starting to fray at the seams now. She dutifully put it on and sat down to make her own broadcast.

They made it out of the engagement with minimal further damage after a tense nineteen hours. When they finally passed the standard six hours without any more peril, everyone went limp with harried relief. Jacklyn lost a minute or two in the captain's chair to exhaustion.

Two decks in Crux Ward had to be evacuated due to hull cracks; an entire library had been punched out of Cygnus Ward. The worst was Perseus Ward: the engagement had taken an enormous bite through several decks. Everyone in them was now drifting through the void, frozen in their eternal mass grave. By the time Jacklyn got down to the affected areas, there were people wailing at sealed-off bulkheads, screaming for the ones who hadn't made it past the internal airlocks in time.

More than one person glared at her as she passed through the ward. Someone even spat. One crew member cornered Jacklyn in a hall and shrieked at her for killing their child, for not jumping out an airlock herself. She waited until they collapsed into sobs before escorting them to their bunk and going topside to make the announcement.

Jacklyn listed the ship's damage and tentative repair plans, but didn't discuss the fact that they were half-blind and who knew what else from Watson's light show. Instead she informed everyone that eulogies would be conducted in the ship's amphitheater during the next shift.

Usually her father made these announcements. She'd had

no idea how difficult they were; deciding what to give and what to withhold from six thousand people waiting beside terminals or datapads to hear their fate was beyond draining. The moment she clicked off the broadcast and shut down her own terminal, she shucked off her uniform and fell into a deep, completely black sleep.

Waking up felt like stepping out of a swamp and into a fog. She didn't feel rested, just numb. There was nothing she could do about that except take her pills, so she dealt with it and made her way down to Sickbay.

The engagement had ruined the plan to jimmy the captain's quarters. Instead, Wang had spent the last day producing a list of the dead and missing. He wasn't in his office when she arrived, so she kept walking until she hit the rehabilitation tanks, where Jolie was bobbing in translucent green healing fluid. Jacklyn wasn't surprised to see that she was challenging Wang's command to stay in the tank.

"The nerves will grow back regardless," Jolie argued, pulling herself up the side of the tank. She was wearing a medical tank top and shorts, which made the burns all along her jaw, throat, and arms stand out in bright, enflamed relief. "I need to get back to work."

"There's nothing for you to do right now," Jacklyn interjected. Even though she had lain down in Jolie's narrow bunk and traded rushed, tired kisses before, she still got flustered when Jolie fixed her dark eyes on her in the doorway. "Why don't you take a few more hours in there?"

A huge sigh whooshed out of Wang. "Thank you, Jack." He threw his hands up and stalked out, giving them some privacy.

"Jack," Jolie greeted her, floating to the near side of the tank. "How's the ship?"

"Not great," Jacklyn said, mouth twisting in a bitter smile. "But repair teams are in place, and vigils are already underway. The only thing left to do is recover."

She considered telling Jolie about the scene in Perseus, about the plummeting morale in every ward, but reached out to wipe gel from Jolie's mouth instead.

Deflating, Jolie let go of the tank and sank back into the medigel, finally submerging her burns as prescribed. "I suppose I can soak for another hour."

Jacklyn cracked a smile. Jolie was still elegant with half the skin from her cheeks to her collarbone shriveled and puckered with soon-to-be scars. "I heard the CMO recommend another five."

Jolie sidestepped that entirely. "You look like you should be in here instead," she observed, taking in the bags under Jacklyn's eyes, the abnormal pallor of her dark skin, the way her braids were loose down her back instead of done up or in her beanie.

Jacklyn managed a weak laugh. They stood in silence for a while, the only sounds the drone of the rehab tank recycling its gel and the beeping of Jolie's vitals from the nearby terminal. Then Jolie pressed her hand to the glass.

"It's not your fault," she said softly.

Jacklyn clenched her jaw. She wished she had the luxury of believing that. But mistakes like these weren't going to get them back home alive.

"I'll do better," she promised, lifting a hand to press to the glass as well.

Jolie nodded, and Jacklyn felt better. They stood on either side of the tank with their hands mirrored for a few more minutes.

"I have to go." Jacklyn pulled back eventually. "There's still something I need to do."

※

Jacklyn tore through Data, radiating a fury that made all the techies shrink away as she stormed straight to Otto's office.

Inside, he had Watson spread across a table like a cadaver. The droid was in pieces with its limbs disconnected and its chassis open again, powered down with its eyes dark and vacant. The stains from the oil streaks down its faceplate made the scene look more sinister than a droid operation.

"I know what you're going to say—" Otto began, but Jacklyn slammed both hands on the table so hard that the shriek of metal scraping the floor cut him off.

"Do you have any idea what you've done?" She only kept her voice down out of respect for the fact that the crew didn't need to hear an argument between officers right now. "We're blind, deaf, and mute. We lost one hundred and fifty-seven people in under twenty-four hours. No less than three separate onboard systems have crashed or been corrupted."

Otto pressed his lips together, drawing in a breath to respond.

"I told you I didn't want your pet on the bridge," she interrupted. "And for good goddamn reasons. We were screwed before—we've been screwed for the last hundred years—but now we might as well be dead." She glanced down at the vacant slouch of Watson's mouth and looked away just as quickly. "I'm terminating this project."

Otto cupped Watson's neck, hunching over it defensively. "You can't! We need Watson more than ever. She's the only way forward now."

"That thing interfered with bridge procedure during an engagement!" Jacklyn hissed.

Otto set his jaw stubbornly. "She was trying to gather data. Her systems were simply too powerful and overloaded the comms."

"What happens when it fries Reclamation and all we have left is shit water to drink?" Jacklyn challenged. "What happens when it shorts the terrarium controls, and the silos and the farms start to rot? What's the point of Watson finding the way forward if we're all already corpses?"

"You're not looking at the big picture," Otto said hotly. "That's exactly the kind of thinking keeping us in this mess."

Jacklyn squeezed the edge of the table hard enough to hurt. "Perseus isn't Watson's fault," she conceded. "But our other problems are. I don't care what you use the droid for—your extra datapad, your creepy little maid—but it won't be interfacing with the *Calypso* anymore."

Color finally flooded Otto's face, a deep red just as angry as she felt. "Your father would understand the importance of this." He sniffed. Jacklyn was about to invite him to knock on the captain's door himself when he added, "Kimberly too."

Jacklyn's lungs seized so tight she couldn't take another breath. The corners of her vision went bright white, and her hands clenched until the skin of her palms split under her nails.

"That droid doesn't leave Data," she whispered. "Not if you still want your position."

She took a step toward the door. Then she spun around and clocked Otto on the jaw, sending him sprawling.

"And don't ever say my sister's name again."

With the bones in her hand creaking in protest, Jacklyn stomped back out of the office. On the way she glimpsed Watson, empty head tilted as if looking at her, oil tears running again.

✳

Jacklyn strode across the hold, rubbing her tired eyes. The atrium of this deck was the tallest on the ship, crisscrossed with catwalks wide enough to fit the cargo carts ferrying ship supplies back and forth. She found the quartermaster already present and directing the relief response to Perseus Ward. He and the other officers and techies swarming the deck looked as run-down and ragged as Jacklyn felt.

"Jack," Panio greeted. "Nice timing."

"Hey," she said hoarsely. "Talk to me about the stores anomaly."

She had just come from Engineering, where she'd found the engineers with their heads together over a holographic table projecting so many different blueprints and plans that the lines blurred together incoherently, their eyes standing out like bruises. Onyekachi had walked her through the destruction uncovered so far. Most of the damage to Sensors had been external, but some life support–adjacent systems were acting oddly. "We've had strange readings in the hold," he had said, rubbing his temples where his dark skin met his bleached-blond curls. "Foodstuffs has complained as well, since the anomalous readings are generated from the silos."

Of all the problems the ship had had over the last hundred years, Jacklyn had never heard of the food systems fluctuating. It might as well happen under her command, she thought bitterly, while the mission was all around taking a turn toward utter failure.

Panio sighed. "There's a wonky terminal by the silos—the numbers are all off. Take a look for yourself." He slapped his cheeks to force himself awake. "I need to make sure the droids are distributing aid in Perseus correctly."

"I'll let you know if I catch anything you guys didn't," Jacklyn said.

As Panio turned toward the lifts, she followed his directions toward the silos terminal, a set of glowing screens that displayed the real-time stats on their current food, air, water, and materials stores. Right away she saw the glitch: the numbers were fluctuating before her eyes, dipping catastrophically low before shooting to pre-Proxima highs, sometimes shorting out altogether.

This was a problem for Systems, but their best and brightest were working themselves to the bone on the bridge; the rest of the department was patching the jagged edges around the gaping wound of Perseus's systems. Maybe she could commandeer a data techie to take a look and offer an opinion, not that she wanted to go anywhere near Otto right now.

She tapped around on the terminal's pull-out keyboard. She was no techie, but she had gone through training just like every other ship-born child. She rooted around in the terminal's innards to see where it was generating the false data and why.

A bang on the wall above the terminal made her heart jump into her throat.

She leaped back against the opposite bulkhead. The noise reverberated down the empty corridor on either side of the terminal while her pulse hammered in her skull.

The hasty seals from the space-bare parts of the ship had surely messed with the internal structure. There was probably more debris knocking around in the ventilation systems that Sanitation had yet to filter. Breathing deep, Jacklyn tried to look for a place where she could open the bulkhead and take a look.

Right as she touched the wall, another bang under her hand made her flinch.

"Buck up," she muttered, trying to get a grip. It was just debris. Sweat beaded at her temples anyway.

Several steps down the corridor was a seam in the bulkhead where a sign announced a maintenance hatch. She rubbed her hands up and down her arms to get rid of the gooseflesh and walked toward it, setting her jaw. If she could identify the noise—

Another bang followed her.

She paused, dragging out her next step as she listened. It was silent for another minute, so she shook the paranoid thoughts out of her head and kept going. She had only taken another few steps when the next bang went off beside her ear.

She spun around to look up and down the corridor. It was still empty. There were several feet between her and the terminal, between the places where the first bang on the wall and the second had struck.

"Debris," she reminded herself weakly. It was natural to get spooked by the *Calypso*'s long, dim corridors, especially now that the ship was running on auxiliary power and perpetually dark, but there was no need to fear things lurking around corners or under panels. That was the trap her mother had fallen into, the one that had ultimately driven her and the crew members that followed her ravings over the edge.

Jacklyn told herself that, but there was nothing made-up about the way another bang came through the bulkhead where she had just been standing. Or the way the next one shook the wall right as she passed by.

They were following her.

"Improper ventilation, faulty sanitation," she listed to herself, but it was too late to keep the shiver from running down her spine. She didn't know of any malfunction that could keep pace like that. She halted in her tracks, unable to make herself go on.

Scuttling around the hold alone in the dark was too unsettling. The simple solution was to come back with Panio or a farm techie to pry open the bulkhead. She turned on her heel to go do just that.

The next bang followed her back the other way.

Jacklyn kicked into a coltish sprint—she couldn't fight the impulse to run, not with her animal hindbrain shouting down her rational mind. She was mortified for only as long as it took the next bang to catch up to her, and the one after that to nip at her heel.

When she hit the lift, she threw herself in and pressed a random button. The lift lurched into motion, carrying her away from the hold. For a moment she thought the sounds would hunt her into the cab, but there was nothing. She leaned against the cool wall of the lift, watching it steam up with her hot breaths.

She had been scared while working in remote corners of the ship before, but not like that. She couldn't calm the panic pulsing through her with each heartbeat, because she didn't have any explanation for what the hell that had been. She fumbled around in her uniform pockets for her datapad to call Viktorija to the hold.

It chimed with an urgent call, startling her badly.

"It's the wards again," Michiko told her, breathing hard and clearly on the move.

"Another riot?" Jacklyn sighed. Her headache intensified, the tension in her body morphing from fear into frustration.

"No," Michiko said. "A mutiny."

Jacklyn waited for the shock to hit her, but apparently she was too exhausted to feel anything other than static at the news. She dropped her head until her braids formed a beaded curtain around her face, breathing in and out slowly. Then she snapped up and rerouted the lift to the bridge.

"Understood. Meet me in the ready room."

4

The bridge repair team had already made strong headway. A group of maintenance droids were replacing the last damaged pieces of the nav station, and the third engineer was putting tourniquets on the amputated comms systems until they could be safely rebooted. The rest of the bridge crew attended their duties seamlessly around the work.

Jolie was back in the captain's chair, medigel strips covering most of the skin above her uniform. Jacklyn beckoned her toward the ready room right away.

"Helm, you have the conn." Jolie fell into step with her. She waited until they were behind closed doors to ask, "What's the situation?"

"A goddamn rebellion," Jacklyn said bluntly.

Jolie's face cycled through grimaces of shock, disbelief, and aggravation before settling on determination. "Understood. What do you know so far?"

Jolie's steadfastness made the ball of anxiety inside Jacklyn's chest collapse and harden into her own kind of resolve. She went to the ready room's enormous conference table. "Michiko will be here soon with more details."

Within the next ten minutes most of the *Calypso*'s brass was gathered around the table. Jacklyn paced at the end while Asher and Jolie conversed in low tones on either side of her. The mission commander bounced her leg next to an equally impatient Viktorija. The head techies of Sensors, Systems, and Life Support were also present; Otto slunk in after them, his swollen cheek earning a few stares. He glanced once in Jacklyn's direction and turned away stiffly. Panio stumbled in a few minutes later, tailed by the ship's purser and director.

Once everyone was seated, Jacklyn stepped up to the head of the table. "Thanks for coming." The faces staring back at her were varied—some curious, some haggard, some annoyed. "I'll get straight to the point: a handful of factions in the wards are in the process of declaring a mutiny."

That jolted the whole table.

"How sophisticated are these factions?" the head life support techie asked anxiously. "If they seize any of the *Calypso*'s systems while they're on the mend, they could do real harm."

"Where are the ward reps?" the head labs techie broke in. "Are they just sitting back and letting this happen?"

Jacklyn held out her hands placatingly as Michiko walked in. "Security can give us more information."

Michiko's face was creased with fatigue. She came around to Jacklyn's side to speak. "Glad you're all here—I'll only have to say this once. At oh four hundred hours, the commons decks of Perseus, Carina, and Cygnus Wards were sealed against all traffic, including essential repair staff. Crux and Orion are the only reps to respond to my hails. Both reported factions among their constituents, which have declared themselves autonomous."

One of the techies swore. Jacklyn felt like doing the same.

"We don't have time for this," Viktorija sighed, crossing her arms. "If we don't finish the structural integrity reviews in Perseus, we could easily lose more pieces of the ward."

"We have to deal with this delicately," the mission commander cautioned. "Whether or not the factions have legitimate concerns, there must be a way to get what everyone wants."

Panio snorted. "I think we all want to live."

"They don't think command is making decisions with ward interests in mind," the director explained.

"We're not," Asher agreed. "We're making decisions with the interest of the entire *Calypso* in mind."

Jacklyn didn't think the logic or validity of the factions was the issue. "What are their demands?"

Michiko slid her datapad to the middle of the table. The fleet's chevron logo spun a few times before the pad chimed and projected a list into the air above the conference table.

The table was quiet as the officers read each item: immediate resource allocation to the wards, a temporary lift on garrison rations, a ward rep station on the bridge to monitor command decisions, etc. Jacklyn considered most of the demands an obstruction to the immediate recovery of the ship, but she wasn't surprised by them.

What she was surprised by was the demand to turn the ship around.

The factions had been independently monitoring the ship's velocity and position in the astronautical charts, and came to the conclusion Jacklyn had been wrestling with every day: the *Calypso* would make it back to Earth as a ghost ship, if it made it back at all.

No one even knew how the humans left on Earth had fared. Carbon dioxide gas percentages, surface temperature, and sea level were higher than they had been for the past several million years. Climate refugees vastly outnumbered war refugees. A mouthful of fresh water was more precious than gold. It had been cheaper to take to the heavens than to try to undo the environmental sins of twenty-first-century capitalism. The *Calypso* might make it back to Earth only to cook in its runaway greenhouse atmosphere. Or they might land only to experience the reckoning of the people who had been abandoned there to die.

A nontrivial number of crew onboard believed their forebears had deserted the Proxima b colony too soon; they already had preliminary plans for improving the colony design, and a secondary plan to extract fuel from Proxima b and test the habitability of the rest of the planetary system.

Most important, the *Calypso* had kept immaculate records of the locations of the engagements they had suffered. By diligently mapping the attacks, the factions had identified a safe path back to Proxima b. They could accelerate and return to the colony within a human lifetime.

Jolie was the first to break the silence in the ready room. "Thorough," she said, almost approvingly.

Jacklyn had to concede that, but there was one thing about the list of demands that rubbed her the wrong way: it was completely, utterly defeatist. She was surprised to hear her thoughts spoken aloud by Otto.

"I'm not convinced," he said. "Would our forebears have made the decision to cross interstellar space again frivolously? No one jumps planets *twice* unless the chances of survival are truly dismal."

The purser spoke up. "It's less about the risk of returning and more about the uncertainty of advancing. Their plan for going back, risky as it is, is a plan; that's more than we can say about our heading so far."

Jacklyn was sorely tempted to debate the choice between

continuing or terminating the mission, but now was not the time. They could discuss that when the factions were no longer holding the most vulnerable parts of the ship hostage. For now, they needed to take action.

"We don't have time to waste," she said loudly, cutting off the chatter. "We have a threat to ship safety to neutralize."

Jolie straightened in her chair. "What do you recommend?"

"I'm opening up the floor to ideas." Jacklyn swept a hand across the table. "First things first, we need to return to repairs or else risk the damage from the last engagement spreading. That means we need to enter negotiations with the factions and post a response to this list. Let's brainstorm—"

She was interrupted by all the lights shutting off.

The ready room went completely black. Even with the ship on half power, the reserve lights should have come on underfoot. The darkness was so sudden and all-consuming that Jacklyn lost her breath. The rest of the table gasped in surprise. Beside her, Jolie reached out blindly and gripped her arm hard.

"Did they just cut power?" Jacklyn asked sharply.

Michiko snatched up her datapad and activated it, providing a little illumination to the room. The blue glow tossed amorphous, elongated shadows on the walls. Jacklyn looked away from the monstrous shapes.

"No, that was a Systems failure," Michiko reported, scrolling quickly. "We should be back up in five, four, three . . ."

When the lights returned, only the emergency ones flashed on. The spare lighting turned everyone's faces into skulls.

"Status report?" Jacklyn asked.

Viktorija was already scrolling through her own datapad. She pulled up a ship schematic and slid it to the center of the table so they could all see. Jacklyn bit her cheek bloody. Asher cursed colorfully, not quite under his breath. One of the techies jumped to their feet.

Everything was wrong.

Gas levels were overall low, and the percentages of CO_2 and argon were wildly out of proportion. Pressure levels were dangerously light on multiple decks, the local air thin enough to jump-start dehydration and tamper with metabolism. Water volumes were pitiful, even taking their hidden cisterns into account. Food stores were a fraction of what they should be, even with the losses from the Perseus evacuation.

Jacklyn felt light-headed. Those levels wouldn't last them through the next decade, let alone the next few centuries. Unless they got the propulsion systems back to the fleet's original performance, they wouldn't even make it back to Proxima b with those resources.

"No," Jacklyn breathed.

The glitch that she had seen on the terminal in the hold must be affecting Viktorija's pad. Otherwise all the talk about dying out here in the void was suddenly a reality. There were no more calculations to do. Only one result remained.

All eyes in the ready room blinked toward her.

"Jack?" Jolie asked quietly. "Any orders?"

Panic shot through Jacklyn like electricity, short-circuiting her nerves. She didn't have any answers. She hadn't done the math for this.

Dad, she prayed instinctively. *Please, come.*

There were so many times when Jacklyn was facing a tough call that her father appeared suddenly with a solution. His ability to inspire confidence in others, to make the room take a collective breath and recover their courage and inspiration—she didn't have that. She didn't know how to foster a sense of community like her mother, nor how to make anyone and everyone smile like her sister. She was the odd Albright out. The helplessness she felt right now, her shortcomings standing out in stark relief, was overwhelming.

In the next moment, however, it was overridden by contempt.

She was an Albright, but she wasn't Noah Albright, who had disappeared and damned the rest of them. She wasn't Tegan Albright, who had let her fear bring death to her long before it would have come on its own. She wasn't Kimberly Albright, since she was still alive.

Jacklyn was the last Albright left. While that was still the case, she had to do what she could.

She looked around the conference table. Her nerves peaked briefly before she settled into her decision.

"We need three teams," she said. "First one is on negotiations. Asher—take point, and whoever you need. Priority is restoring ward access to emergency repair staff." She was gratified when Asher nodded and grabbed his datapad, the mission commander and the director getting to their feet with him.

"The other teams will investigate our stores," she continued, stronger. "We need to know if these stats are correct. Department heads—keep your people focused on debugging." She received nods from all the techies.

"Panio—you'll have to open the stores directly. I want to confirm all the silos are secure." He gave a thumbs-up and rose with the purser.

"I'll go with Michiko down to Security to monitor the mutiny." Jacklyn took a deep breath. This next order would be the most contentious and most likely to be questioned. "Viktorija, tell Kachi to prepare the propulsion system. If those numbers are right . . . we're going to have to jump."

Once again the whole table jolted. Every face turned to look at her incredulously, but this time Jacklyn didn't feel self-conscious.

Viktorija closed her dropped jaw. "You want to space jump, Jack?"

Jacklyn certainly did not, not after all the times Onyekachi had complained about the sorry state of their shock absorbers. But they didn't have a choice. "Whether we go forward or backward, we have to jump," she reasoned. "There's no way we'll make it to Earth or Proxima b otherwise."

When none of the others tried to make a counterargument, she gestured toward the door. "Let's get to it. Jolie, you have the conn."

Once the room emptied out, Michiko looked at Jacklyn appraisingly. "Not bad, Jack."

Jacklyn rubbed her nape, somehow pleased. "I'm trying."

Michiko left the ready room for the next lift down, already reviewing the reports coming in on her pad. Right as Jacklyn went to follow, Jolie caught the sleeve of her uniform, holding her back until they were alone.

She used her grip to turn Jacklyn so they were facing each other. Then she rocked onto her toes so she could press a swift, precise kiss to the corner of her mouth.

"Oh." Jacklyn blushed. "What was that for?"

"We'll get this situation under control," Jolie said, smirking at Jacklyn's flustered face. "Just be safe until then."

"You got it," Jacklyn murmured, dipping her head to return the favor.

Jolie only stood still long enough to let Jacklyn caress her hurt cheek before turning toward the door with a whip of her dark hair and leaving to take command again.

Alone, Jacklyn squeezed her eyes shut and wondered if she was doing any of this right. Then she fixed her braids and left to join the work.

✳

Jacklyn pressed the lift button for Security. Michiko had a room full of live feeds from cameras and sensors around the ship. Chances were the factions had cut the feeds to their locations, but even dark spots among the fly-eyed, multi-faceted view could reveal details about their movement and breadth.

She was about to message regarding the factions' whereabouts when the whole lift shook.

Jacklyn nearly tumbled to the floor, grabbing the railing at the last moment. A metallic squeal made her clap her free hand over her ear—it was the lift grinding along the side of the shaft, somehow tilted and knocked off of its track. It only made it down a few more feet before the emergency brake kicked in and halted its descent.

"Of course," Jacklyn sighed, rubbing her shoulder where she had been jostled against the wall. She waited a few moments, but for some reason the balancing mechanism on the lift didn't tilt it back to its proper position. She jumped a few times to try forcing it upright manually—no dice. She took out her pad to see if there were any nearby maintenance droids, hitting send on a request.

Something banged on the top of the lift.

Jacklyn blanched. Sliding her pad back into her pocket, she stared up at the ceiling. The lift's counterweight was at the bottom, not the top. The shaft wasn't connected to Ventilation or Reclamation; there was no way it could be debris. Either one of the metallic strands of the lift's enormous cable had snapped, or something had fallen on top.

Another bang shuddered the lift, this one on the ceiling hatch.

More fraying on the cable? Something else falling down? Jacklyn didn't like either of those possibilities. The creaking and scraping of the lift against the shaft walls made unease bubble in her guts. She leaned on the button for the lift doors; when she got a notification that the lift was between floors, she input an override and forced the doors open.

She was stuck halfway between the labs deck and the command quarters deck. There was just enough room for her to pull herself onto the former by her fingernails and squeeze through the opening. She deliberated whether she wanted to risk being cut in half by the lift falling while she was shimmying out or waste valuable time stuck in here waiting for a droid to help.

The handle for the ceiling hatch wiggled.

Jacklyn froze. She stared at the handle in disbelief, watching it carefully for several moments. When it shook again, her heart kicked into high gear. She backed against the wall as the jiggling intensified. Soon the handle was clanging against the hatch, sending up a horrible racket that made her hands clammy.

Jacklyn told herself not to leap to fantastical, doomsday explanations like her mother, but what else was there? That was no cable or fallen part. A techie doing work on the cab? They would have shut down the whole shaft. Something was jerking the handle from the outside. That made her decision for her—she started to pry herself frantically out of the lift.

The whole thing groaned as she crawled through the gap, turning her fear into outright panic. She managed to claw her way onto the labs deck without incident, so spooked that she stumbled upright and put several feet between her and the lift opening.

She started to breathe a sigh of relief until the lift shook with another bang. Despite the emergency brake, the vibrations made the lift cab inch downward. The next bang slid the lift down again, and the one after that. Jacklyn watched, petrified, as the knocks on the top of the lift slowly jimmied it farther and farther down its cable.

The top of the lift was almost level with the labs deck.

Jacklyn lunged for the lift panel, stabbing the screen until the doors whooshed closed and blocked the lift from sight.

With a barrier between her and the banging, Jacklyn regained her composure. She exhaled shakily and turned to find another way downship, promising herself she would think about what the hell had just happened later. Paranoid, she was still looking back when she started walking, unwilling to take her eyes off the seam of the door.

Facing the wrong way, she walked straight into Watson.

The collision sent her sprawling. Watson, on the other hand, barely budged from its stance in the middle of the corridor.

"You," Jacklyn seethed, rubbing her chest where Watson's faceplate had struck her hard. "What the hell are you doing outside Data?"

Watson's false hair had been reglued and the melted skin of its forearms replaced with temporary silicon sleeves. The oil tracks had been wiped from its faceplate, leaving no trace.

The droid gave an exaggerated blink, something that Jacklyn had never seen before. "The doctor let me out."

For a long moment Jacklyn scrutinized it. It stared back at her with an expression so bland that it made her suspicious. After a few seconds she asked incredulously, "Did you just lie?"

Watson looked like it was going to argue. Instead it gave up and shrugged stiffly. "I tried."

Jacklyn had never heard a droid lie before; she should have expected that it was possible, especially for an android. "Why are you here?" she demanded. If Watson thought it could roam the ship freely after its stunt, it had another think coming.

"I heard your message for help," the droid replied. "So I came."

Jacklyn's eyebrows flew up. She glanced down at her datapad where she had sent a notification about the lift malfunction. "You were listening to my pad?"

"I've been listening to all the ship's pads," Watson corrected. Jacklyn spasmed at that, though it shouldn't be surprising after the droid had demonstrated the capacity to handle a shift's worth of the *Calypso*'s entire data input. "I detected several locations onboard where I could be useful. I'm sorry for what happened on the bridge, Jack. I was just trying to help."

Jacklyn had a million questions for the droid: What nonsense had it been spouting during its yellow-eyed fit, why had it touched the comms console, why did it lie about being let out? Unfortunately they didn't even have time for one. "We'll discuss this later. Follow me."

She couldn't make another stop to put the droid somewhere out of the way; it would have to stay close to her for now. She jogged across the dark deck, Watson keeping up obediently.

"Jack," it said apologetically when they arrived at the other lift. "I don't think you can use this one."

"Why not?" Jacklyn pressed the lift button a few times, but it didn't respond. Its panel wasn't even flashing a current status or location. "What the hell?"

She thought about forcing the doors, but the memory of the inexplicable jiggling hatch in the other lift made her reconsider.

"I used this one to come here," Watson admitted. "I believe I accidentally overloaded it."

Jacklyn was ready to tear her braids out one by one. "New rule: don't touch *anything* else. Not until Otto dumps those stupid upgrades."

"I don't want the doctor to take them out," Watson said immediately.

"Tough luck," Jacklyn retorted. "Right now you're a danger to ship safety."

"You can remove them," the droid clarified. "But not him."

Jacklyn stalled. She hadn't expected that. Watson had always been so docile with Otto. Then again, she remembered the looks on its face the last few times she had seen it splayed open on his table.

"We'll discuss that later too," she said quietly. "Right now we need to find another way off this deck."

Besides the lifts, the only way to move between decks was the maintenance hatches; Jacklyn had worked on one just a few days ago—the one where she had first heard the sounds in the walls. They would have to try that.

"Come on," she said, leading them back in that direction.

The closer they got to the hatch, however, the slower Watson approached. Jacklyn glanced behind her to find Watson still a ways down the corridor. "What's the problem?" she called, annoyed.

"There's an anomaly," Watson reported. The droid's face was drawn with concern. It was getting better at emoting.

Somehow that made Jacklyn more uncomfortable than the overheating hypodroid from last time. "So I've heard. In the wall, right?"

Watson shook its head. "In the hatch."

Jacklyn frowned. She looked down at the floor, almost waiting to hear the banging sounds from before. When the silence continued, she steeled herself and grabbed the handle. There was only one way to go.

She opened the hatch.

And immediately recoiled.

"Jack?"

There was a body in there.

Right away she knew it was dead. The stench was surprisingly subtle, probably because the corridors were so cold.

But the position was wrong, and the color was wrong, and the blood and guts were on the wrong side of the skin.

Jacklyn put her hand over her mouth, worried she was going to be sick. She had seen corpses before—that was the reality of war, even if they were just the ones caught in a cosmic crossfire beyond their perception—but never with their viscera hanging out like the wires of an opened console. Tegan's body had just been stiff and pale. Not even Kimberly, who died from being juiced, had looked like this afterward.

The face was vaguely familiar, but she didn't recognize the person until she saw the Cygnus Ward tattoo on his neck. It was Vidal.

"Shit," Jacklyn whispered behind her hand.

Why was he here? *How* was he here? When she had left the hatch a few days ago, it had been empty. Viktorija had said Vidal went to the machine shops for more epoxy. What the hell could have gone wrong on that kind of errand?

Jacklyn closed the hatch, trying not to disturb his body. She yanked out her datapad and tapped on it with shaking fingers.

"You told the CMO?" Watson said, closer now. The look on its face was faraway as it listened to her communications again.

"Something's wrong here," Jacklyn replied, clearing her throat when she heard how high and tight her voice came out. "I need a medical officer to look at this."

It took a while for someone to reach them. Maintenance droids were already working on both of this deck's stalled lifts, so the ship's coroner had to get off a deck below and climb up another hatch.

They greeted Jacklyn solemnly. "What are we dealing with, Jack?"

Jacklyn opened the hatch for them, turning her head so she wouldn't have to see again. She was impressed at the way the coroner merely grimaced before kneeling down for a closer look. They recorded the pallor of Vidal's skin, the size of his pupils, the color and texture of his blood where it had congealed down the sides of the hatch.

"I'd like a second opinion," they said after a long, silent examination. "But I can tell you mine right now. He died from evisceration and exsanguination, and he's missing a few organs. I'll need Wang to corroborate, but this can't have been an accident, or self-inflicted.

"This was an act of murder."

5

By the time a body bag and extra medical officers showed up, Jacklyn had called Michiko. The timing was too suspect. Vidal's death—the *Calypso*'s first murder in half a century—coming right as the factions announced themselves made her assume the worst. Anyone could be at risk if the factions were willing to kill to get what they wanted.

Michiko's waning patience was audible through the pad speakers. "What would they gain by killing an engineer from one of their own wards?"

"I'm not sure," Jacklyn admitted. "All I know is this problem just became much more complicated."

She contacted the negotiations team after that. Asher answered her call. "Jack. We're in the middle of talks with a Perseus faction. Can we—"

"Someone's been murdered." She cut right to the chase. "We need to halt negotiations until we know who's responsible."

"Good god—" The director's voice echoed tinnily down the line.

"An engineer from Cygnus," Jacklyn continued. "I . . . found him in a maintenance hatch on the labs deck. The coroner said it's foul play."

"I just want one break," the mission commander grumbled in the background.

"So we can't proceed until we rule out the factions'

involvement," Asher sighed. Jacklyn knew from experience that he was chewing the skin of his lip.

"Priority's still getting access to repairs," she said, "but now we have grounds to do so by force if they refuse to cooperate."

By force Jacklyn meant a security team equipped with magnetic cuffs and low-voltage electrified barriers. Security had more powerful gear, but Jacklyn had no intention of contributing to further violence. "I'll get back to you with Michiko's recommendation," she said, ending the call.

"Jack," Watson suddenly said. The droid had been assisting the medical officers with Vidal's removal, making sure not to drop any viscera. They put his guts in a separate box for transport and placed the rest of him in the bag. Now that they had left in one of the repaired lifts, Watson returned to Jack's side.

She had a hard time looking away from its blood-smeared hands. "What is it?"

"I don't think the factions are responsible," it said. "There's been no mention of Vidal in their internal communications."

Jacklyn didn't know whether to be grateful for Watson's omniscience or uncomfortable. "That could be deliberate," she countered. "Or maybe the deed was done by a subset of the factions to leverage their cause."

"It was something else," Watson insisted. "The thing behind the door."

Jacklyn was surprised enough that she finally looked up at the droid's face. She grimaced when she saw its eyes were glowing that wrong, jaundiced color again.

"Jack, the factions are getting impatient since we went radio silent," Asher said through the pad. "What is Michiko's recommendation?"

Jacklyn checked, but Security had offered no response yet. "Sorry. Stand by." She ended the call on his annoyed noise and looked hard at Watson.

"What's wrong with your eyes?" she asked. "What door are you talking about? What thing behind it?"

"It's inside the fleet," Watson answered. "In every flotilla. In all of the ships. I heard it."

"Heard what?" The haunting noise that Watson had spouted in Data popped up in Jacklyn's mind. "You mean the signal?"

Watson shook its head. "I can't understand *them* yet. I heard the thing behind the door myself. The other ships made the mistake of opening theirs."

"Make some goddamn sense!" Jacklyn blurted. "Who is *them*? What's in the ships?"

Asher interjected, "Jack, we need something quick, or else they're going to cut us off."

Jacklyn closed the connection without responding and tried to call Michiko directly—it didn't go through. A frisson of worry curled through her. She was on edge with all this vague talk of doors and hidden things.

"Jack." The chime of a new call snapped her out of her thoughts.

She swiped at her pad, surprised to see Wang on the line. "Yeah, go."

"The coroner just dropped off Vidal's body," he announced. "I can already confirm their conclusion."

"You found something else?" Jacklyn guessed.

He sounded too strange for this to be a simple second

opinion; there was a tremor in his voice that only poured oil on the spreading conflagration of Jacklyn's apprehension.

"Yes," he answered. She could hear him lick his lips nervously. "He wasn't killed by anyone onboard."

Jacklyn was dumbfounded. "What the hell do you mean? You just said he was murdered."

"He was," Wang said, stressing his next words. "I'm saying it wasn't one of the crew."

Jacklyn was going to do something violent too if the people around her didn't stop talking in mysteries. "How do you know that? Who else could it have been—?"

She stopped short. The corridor air felt especially cold with her blood turning to ice in her veins. She looked at Watson, still staring at her with those gallstone eyes.

". . . There's someone else on the ship?"

Wang made a noise in the affirmative. "I think we have an intruder."

***

Jolie stood up when Jacklyn burst onto the bridge, shocked to see her again so soon. Her greeting disintegrated when Watson exited the lift behind her. "What is the droid doing here?" she asked warily.

"We have a bigger problem," Jacklyn said, bypassing the captain's chair. She stopped at the systems station, where the head techie was rebooting the console with a look of pride. Her assistants parted like mice as Jacklyn stalked into their midst.

"Jack," she said excitedly. "We managed to cut out most of

the Systems necrosis. The helm is unlocked and nav should be ready to deploy shortly."

"Great work," Jacklyn said impatiently, feeling bad for the way the techie's shoulders dropped but unable to waste time on apologizing. "What about the stats for supplies?"

"We routed out the glitch," the techie said quietly. "But the stats haven't changed."

Jacklyn barely even felt that blow, her mind still going a light-year a minute. "Can you show me a map of bio-signs onboard?"

Taken aback, the techie pulled up a ship schematic, this time with infrared data overlaid. Thousands of little dots appeared on the hologram, each one representing a crew member. At this scale they were packed tightly like stars in a globular cluster, too tiny to see individually.

"Zoom in on the hold," Jacklyn said, hoping her hunch wasn't correct.

She had thought about what Wang had said on the way up here. If there was someone else on-ship, they must have had a way to remain hidden from the crew while retaining access to the necessities for survival. They would be in a remote part of the ship with sustenance nearby. One place fit the bill.

The scale of the schematic shrunk. Now the infrared dots were big enough that each one was visible and labeled with that person's crew number. She could see a few people holed up in the quartermaster's office, as well as various teams moving supplies in and out of the stores. She could even see Panio and the purser on their way to the silos, stopping periodically to check terminals as they went.

"Zoom in again," Jacklyn said, her mouth drying up.

By now others could see it too. The ship had eight silos ringing the hold, each one as big around as a whole ward. They held the sealed and shrunken stores of supplies that sustained the *Calypso*'s population. Two silos read empty. That was no glitch—they had been used up by the colonists during their attempt to make a home on Proxima b. Another one read half-full, which Jacklyn could also vouch for, as a previous captain had authorized its depletion after a poor harvest from the farms a few decades ago. There was a fourth silo, however, that was blinking on low even though it should've been as full as the day it was packed for the *Calypso*'s launch.

Inside that silo was a red dot.

There was no crew number attached to it.

"There's our intruder," Jacklyn declared.

The bridge crew, who had been eavesdropping, recoiled at the word. Stunned, the techie blurted, "Intruder . . . ?"

The crew staring over at the systems station were too professional to erupt with questions, but the air on the deck became taut enough to snap. Jolie seized Jacklyn's shoulder and spun her around, hissing, "What the hell is going on, Jack?"

The chime of Jacklyn's datapad broke the aghast silence. She gave the conn to the helm and dragged Jolie into the ready room. Watson tagged along like a leashed dog.

"Sorry for the delay," Michiko said breathlessly. "There's been pushback from nonfaction crew members about their decks being repurposed for a mutiny. We've had to clean up some all-out brawls."

There was no easy way to update Michiko, so Jacklyn just

dumped the info all at once. "The CMO confirmed the murder, and said it wasn't the work of any other crew member. I just found an intruder in our silos. What do you advise?"

Silence reigned on the line for nearly a minute. Jacklyn didn't blame Michiko, since even Jolie looked lost right now. Nothing like this had ever happened in the *Calypso*'s long history.

When Michiko finally responded, her voice was admirably even. "I recommend a ship-wide quarantine. The factions are already sealed in the wards. Get the rest of the crew back in their bunks until we have the intruder in custody. After that we can investigate the murder, and then deal with the mutiny."

The rapid-fire priority changes made Jacklyn dizzy, but she answered in the affirmative. "Panio is down in the hold right now—I'll tell him not to engage until we have a plan."

"I'll come with a team of whoever I haven't already deployed," Michiko promised. "Since the circumstances are extenuating, I'm coming armed."

Nobody had ever been armed on-ship, not since their forebears developed a robust program of alternatives to heavy disciplinary tactics. Jacklyn held out hope that they could subdue the intruder before using any of the real weapons in the security deck's locker.

She went to the terminal at the head of the room and cleared her throat before turning on the intercom that would spread her voice to every corner of the ship.

"Attention, crew," Jacklyn said, heart pounding. "Intruder alert. Ship-wide quarantine effective immediately. Off-duty crew must return to quarters until quarantine is lifted. Ship-essential crew may remain at stations, but department doors must be locked. I repeat, all crew members must follow heavy quarantine protocol."

All the way up in the ready room, there was no way for her to know how the rest of the ship had taken that announcement. Probably with less composure than the bridge crew. As soon as she turned off the intercom, Jolie assaulted her with questions.

"Who was murdered?" she asked. "What kind of intruder are we talking about?"

"A Cygnus Ward engineer," Jacklyn said, taking out her datapad and tapping through the crew contacts. "Wang said no crew member could have killed Vidal."

"How could he determine that?" Jolie asked incredulously. "In order for an intruder to survive undetected on the ship for this long . . . ! The last time the *Calypso* could have possibly picked up a stowaway was on Proxima b."

"Wang said—" Jacklyn had to stop and clear her throat. She couldn't believe she was about to say the words, but they had come to her straight from the CMO. "Wang said that the fatal wound Vidal received wasn't made with any tool that exists on the ship. Whatever killed him did so with something . . . organic."

Jolie looked ill. Jacklyn felt bad for giving her the gory details—she didn't even eat the false meat served by the galley staff. "By organic, you mean—?"

"They found something like keratin filaments in the wounds," Jacklyn clarified. "The protein's all wrong—it's different from our hair or nails—but apparently it resembles the stuff in tetrapod claws."

Jolie started pulling strands of her long hair into a nervous braid. Jacklyn hesitated before giving her the rest.

"He also said that Vidal's missing organs had jagged edges consistent with mark patterns from some kind of jaw. They were bitten out." She paused at Jolie's horrified exhale. "But the teeth marks and the keratin analog don't match anyone on the ship. Don't match, um, anything on the ship."

Jolie looked at her like she was speaking in tongues. "Jack. What are you saying?"

Watson spoke suddenly from its place near the door, startling both of them. The plaintive urgency in its voice was so human and real that Jacklyn felt a shot of alarm.

"They're opening the door!" it wailed.

"What door?" Jacklyn asked, grabbing Watson by its thin shoulders. The droid was so petite it looked like she should be able to toss it over her shoulder, but it was denser than any human and stood rigid against her tugs. That was disappointing, because she wanted to shake it until a real explanation fell out of it for once.

Instead of responding, Watson popped its jaw apart, opening its mouth in that too-wide yawn. Instead of vomiting static, it spoke in human voices, some of which Jacklyn knew personally.

"—Flotilla, this is the *Gaea*. If anybody else is listening out there . . . sssss . . . in the ship. We have . . . from the colony—ssss—ssss—heard the re . . . from the *Nezha* and the *Paradise Lost*. Do not open—"

"—the *Ptesan Win*. Who's left? If you have . . . it's—ssss—sssssssssssssssssssss—something in here—"

"Come in? We're . . . the *Mami Wata*. The captain of the *Ishtar* said—ssss—ssss—the whole crew, gone—"

"Please, anybody—! The *Bast* and the *Itzpapalotl* are missi—sssssssssssssss—end help! It's on the inside—"

"How did you . . . ?" Jacklyn whispered. Those were transmissions from other ships in the Goddess Flotilla. They hadn't received a clear message in months—yet Watson was playing them loud and crisp. "You got these from the comms console?"

The droid continued puking out the cleaned-up recordings. Jacklyn heard virtually the same message over and over again, from ships like the *Ostara* and the *Durga* and the *Banu Goshasp*.

"They were in peril," Jolie noted as the transmissions continued to spool out of Watson's cranked mouth. "From something inside the ships—"

Jacklyn thought of the blank red dot sitting in the middle of the half-empty silo. She thought of Vidal's crumpled body, dangling its innards like fruits and vines from some grotesque tree. She thought of the warning she had heard ten times over now.

She dashed back to the table to scoop up her datapad. She pressed the wrong screens twice in her hurry before she was finally able to make the urgent call she needed.

"Panio, come in," she shouted. "Hold your position. Stay away from the silos! There's something dangerous in there—*don't open the door.*"

There was no response. The fleet's chevron spun on the screen before it went dark with inactivity. Jacklyn growled and tried again. No answer. Dread clogged her throat, making it hard to breathe around the worry that she was too late.

She was struck with a better idea. "Watson." She spun back to the droid. "You can listen to his pad, right? What do you hear?"

Watson concentrated for a moment. Then, right in front

of Jacklyn, the blue glow of its eyes festered into that queasy yellow. Its brow knotted and its mouth twisted into a perfect visage of fear. All that emotion on its broken faceplate made Jacklyn lean back.

"What is it?" she pressed, feeling all wrong.

Watson opened its mouth again. Instead of signals detected from the ship's external sensors, it transmitted the internal data from the feeds and open terminals in the hold. As soon as the live noise came through, Jolie grabbed Jacklyn's wrist so hard she felt it might break; Jacklyn covered her mouth with the other hand. They listened to the transmission with nauseating horror.

It was the sound of screams.

※

Jacklyn made it down to the hold deck right as Michiko made it up. Watson was at Jacklyn's heels, making the deck floor shake with every heavy step as they ran from the lift to the atrium. They converged with the security team, whose uniforms had been covered with aramid fiber vests, coming from the opposite direction. The voltage prods latched to their belts and the plasma guns slung across their shoulders, the first weapons Jacklyn had ever really seen, were menacing but necessary, depending on what they found in the silos.

They all sprinted down the gangway toward the unidentified red dot. Screams echoed in Jacklyn's ears as they got closer and closer to where Watson had been listening. She struggled to block out thoughts of what could have torn those noises out, but the memory of Vidal's corpse was stark and terrible in her mind.

She cradled the hope that they would get there in time like a hand around a tiny, guttering flame, but when they finally skidded to a stop in front of the compromised silo, that hope was snuffed out.

On the ground were Panio and the purser.

Jacklyn retched at the sight and scent. Guilt climbed her gullet; she had to swallow again and again to keep from throwing up. Her crewmates were in pieces, afloat in a puddle of their still-warm blood. She gagged so hard that her eyes teared.

Michiko set her jaw. Wasting no time, she split her officers into two teams and stationed one beside the bodies.

"Check for signs of life," she ordered the first. "Keep sights on the door. We're going in." She took the second team through the enormous open doors of the silo; beyond the threshold was utter darkness. The lights inside the storage vat were all off.

Jacklyn made herself watch as two officers dropped dutifully to the deck, blood soaking their uniforms through the knees and shins. She already knew from the vacant, half-lidded gapes on both of the blood-flecked faces what they would find; she closed her eyes when they both shook their heads.

There was nothing to do except call the coroner's team again. While she tapped her pad, the security officers fanned out from the corpses and took up positions around the silo entrance. Michiko and the other team had already disappeared into the huge space. Jacklyn could only wait in tense, miserable silence for them to return with news of the intruder—or engage with it.

The whole time they were gone Jacklyn was afraid the

screaming would start again in the depths of the silo. The coroner had already taken the bodies away, not quite as unflappable this time in the face of fresh, brutal gore. Jacklyn didn't know what she would do if she had to call them yet again.

Michiko was gone long enough that the blood on the ground started to congeal, and sanitation droids from Life Support arrived to clean the mess. Jacklyn got antsy.

She turned to Watson. "Can you hear the intruder? Are they still in the silo?"

"No," Watson said. Its eyes glowed blue again. "They're currently not in any place on the ship with a live feed or sensors."

Jacklyn frowned. How many places on the ship could an intruder hide from all internal sensors? Every bunk, department, corridor, and commons had security cameras, heat or motion detectors, or all of the above. The only locations where the fleet's architect hadn't deigned to put sensors were inside the walls—

Jacklyn sucked in a shaky breath.

The anomaly.

Michiko and her team finally returned. "There's no sign of the intruder," she declared, exiting the silo. "Just loads of missing stores and traces of their squatting."

"Traces?" Jacklyn echoed. Another material sample from the intruder could tell them something important. The biology lab had been destroyed in the engagement before last, but its researchers were working out of Sickbay. "Did you get a—"

"Right here," Michiko said, already ahead of her.

"I think the intruder is using the walls to get around the ship," Jacklyn reported, taking Michiko's recovered sample.

"They'll be damn hard to track, then," Michiko sighed. She gestured for a few officers to seal the silo again, and told the ones who had posted a lookout to do a careful sweep of the deck anyway. "When you've dropped that off, meet me in my office."

※

Jacklyn jolted awake from where she was leaned against the wall of the repurposed surgery theater where the bio team was currently holed up. She must have fallen asleep sometime during the team's long analysis of the silo sample—the shocked cry that came from the techies working on it under their microscopic, chromatographic, and electrochemical tools jerked her back upright.

"Jack." The head labs techie rushed over. "This is extraordinary."

"What did you find?" Jacklyn asked, thinking she might already know the answer.

"This sample doesn't resemble any known biospecimen," the techie reported. "There is no genetic evidence that whatever made this sample evolved on the same planet as us."

Jacklyn already had the implication dangling in front of her face, but it was still difficult to articulate. She bit the bullet and said the words out loud.

"You're saying this sample came from something . . . not from Earth."

The researchers tittered in the background. The techie nodded wildly. "This is the first direct evidence of extraterrestrial life."

Jacklyn wished she had time to marvel at the discovery.

She wished she could sit down at the very least. But they couldn't just sit on this; they needed to act. "From the colony?"

"The fleet has only ever been to one other world," they pointed out.

Until her death Jacklyn's mother had never stopped talking about fairy tales, the kind of juvenile stories that had cropped up in nurseries on Proxima b. Tales of monsters that dug their way up from beneath the sun-scorched, irradiated ground to steal children from the colony, dragging them away from the terminator either to roast them in searing daylight or suck their bones clean in deep, impenetrable night. Jacklyn had liked the stories as a kid.

Hearing Tegan tell them earnestly as an adult had been embarrassing, even disturbing. Though life on Proxima b had never been confirmed, her mother had warned her again and again before her suicide that the Centauri monsters would get them in the end. One time she had locked both her daughters in her bunk and preached for hours about monsters on the ship; her eyes had been so big and her lips pulled back so wide that Jacklyn had stood in front of Kimberly the whole time. Their father had eventually broken in and taken Tegan down to Sickbay for an evaluation and prescription that ultimately hadn't worked.

Jacklyn closed her eyes. In the end, her mother had been right.

According to the messages that Watson had played, every ship in the fleet might have been infested. Who knew how many had inadvertently opened their intruders' hiding places and unleashed them into their midst? How many crews had been hunted and devoured already?

Jacklyn shook as she realized how close she had come, on several occasions, to going the way of Vidal or Panio. Every time she had heard the banging, she had only been a bulkhead away from spilling her blood and guts across the deck.

She asked Watson, "Can you send a transmission to the rest of the flotilla? If anybody is still out there, they need to know."

Watson acquired a faraway look as it cycled through different comms channels. Eventually the droid shook its head. "No one is responding, Jack. Either they've already heard the previous warnings, or there is no one else to warn anymore."

"Right," Jacklyn said, rubbing her face. "Before we worry about other ships, we need to take care of our own." There was an extraterrestrial intruder stalking through the *Calypso*'s walls, and the longer they took to find it, the greater the chance it would strike again. "We have to go on the hunt."

❋

Jacklyn and Watson found Michiko in her office as ordered. Once all of her officers were accounted for, they sealed the deck and completed a mini briefing. Michiko repeated the bio team's findings.

"Sir," one of the officers said dubiously. "You're saying . . . there's an alien onboard."

"You're free to double-check the research," Michiko said imperiously. She pulled up pictures of Panio from the coroner on her datapad and projected her screen for the whole room to see. "Take a look at these and tell me if you think that's a priority right now."

Several officers blanched. Even Jacklyn, who had been on the scene herself, had to look away. There were no more outbursts after that.

"Our responsibility is ship safety only," Michiko said. "Not astrobiology, not taxonomy. It doesn't matter what this thing is—we need to find and subdue it before it takes any more of our people."

She laid out the standards for the op: they would break into teams assigned to different regions of the ship and seal all doors, vents, and lift shafts on each deck. General orders included escorting any crew in defiance of quarantine to sealed spaces and subduing any faction activity threatening quarantine protocol. As for the intruder, they were to proceed with extreme prejudice.

"I want everyone suited up just in case any more systems fail," she added. "The more decks we seal, the more Earth-normal conditions onboard will deteriorate. That might take out our problem for us, but we can't take that chance. Head to the armory."

The officers filed out of the office and took the gangway to the deck's weapons locker. Before today it hadn't been opened since the colonists had fled back to the stars. Jacklyn felt a morbid curiosity about its contents, but instead of following she used the opportunity for privacy to make a call to the bridge crew.

"Go, Jack," Jolie answered.

"I want you guys to suit up," Jacklyn said. "Pressurized suit, helmet, air tanks. I think the intruder is getting around in the walls. You need to seal the lift doors *and* the vents to the bridge, so nothing gets up there."

Jacklyn expected Jolie's usual coolheaded cooperation.

She was surprised when Jolie asked sharply, "And what about you? Are you still with Michiko?"

"I'm joining security's hunt for the intruder," Jacklyn confirmed. "We're going to take this thing down before it kills us off like the rest of the fleet."

She had to wait several moments for a response. She could hear Jolie hand over the conn and beat a swift retreat to the ready room. Jolie finally spoke when she was equally alone.

"Don't be a martyr," she said icily. "You're the first mate. Get back to the bridge and leave the firefight to the professionals."

Somehow Jacklyn smiled. "I'm no martyr. You and Asher keep coordinating things on top—I'll make my way back up there eventually."

"You'd better," Jolie threatened.

Jacklyn almost felt bad for enjoying the worry in her voice. It was nice to know that she wasn't the only one who considered their off-duty encounters more than just passing the eternity in space with another warm body.

"No matter what," she told Jolie seriously, "keep us going forward. There is no going back to Proxima b now. Any remaining colonists probably already met their fates. We can't let that happen here."

"Understood," Jolie said. Right before she signed off, she murmured, "Come back, Jack."

"Yes, sir," Jacklyn whispered, cutting the call.

She took a few deep breaths. It was hard to overcome the sudden fear that she was going on a suicide mission. Anything that evolved on Proxima b must be tough, since the colonists could barely survive on the exoplanet's surface even with technological assistance. They would have a hard time getting the intruder before it got them.

There was one thing left to do before she joined the security officers for the hunt. She went to the terminal in the live feed room to make another ship-wide announcement.

"Attention all crew members. Quarantine has now been elevated to lockdown. Suit up in emergency gear and completely seal off doors and vents to your location. Do not violate lockdown protocol for any reason until given the all-clear. Make sure you are space-ready in case of onboard systems failure. I repeat, do not exit your location for any reason. Your life depends on it."

6

Jacklyn wasn't used to being suited up. The extra weight was burdensome. Her helmet blocked her peripheral vision, which strummed a low chord of anxiety in her chest. The gun strapped to her suit made her feel worse instead of better. The only training she had with the weapon was the ten-minute version that Michiko had just given everybody else.

She was part of the team assigned to the bow. Michiko hadn't wanted Jacklyn on any team at all—she had pulled her aside to argue extensively against her presence. Asher was still trying to resume essential repairs, Jacklyn had pointed out, while Jolie was making sure they didn't go floating belly-up in the interstellar sea. She was the only one without her hands tied.

"I can keep Jack safe," Watson had piped up to add. Jacklyn was blindsided by the support.

Michiko wasn't impressed. "Aren't you a data droid?"

"I have eyes and ears on all parts of the *Calypso*," Watson pressed. "I can help."

Michiko had weighed the time cost of the argument against the urgent need to protect the ship, and walked away with a sigh.

Now Jacklyn was at the top of the ship, one of five team members assigned to a senior officer named Yanis. Of all the members of her team, she was the most familiar with the upper decks, so they put her right behind the team leader as they cautiously exited the lift and crept onto the control deck with their plasma guns drawn.

The hunt had begun.

"Watson," Jacklyn murmured into her helmet's comms. She spoke on the team's direct line to avoid any noise besides the shuffle of boots on the gangway. "See anything?"

Watson didn't move its mouth but instead sent its reply directly to her headset. "There is nothing in view of the sensors. The intruder may be present and hiding in a bulkhead."

Jacklyn knew that very well. Instead of responding she followed Yanis's gesture forward.

The control deck was slightly bigger than the bridge, which sat at the very nose of the *Calypso*. The latter only comprised the helm and ready room. The former, on the other hand, housed the mates' office, the mission commander's office, and both the Astronautics and Avionics departments. That was a lot of ground to cover, especially since each space was dimly lit with only reserve power, and full of the nooks and crannies that came with bureaucracy.

They began with the mates' office, filing in weapons first. Yanis waved a hand in front of the lights panel, but the office, which was divided into three sections, remained grimly dark. The techies must have missed this malfunction—or maybe it wasn't an accident. Jacklyn remembered how, during the times she had heard the anomaly, the hypo-droid had overheated, how the observation deck detectors had stopped working, how the terminal down in the hold had glitched.

"Behind this bulkhead is the third mate's station," Jacklyn said quietly. "Then the second's, and then mine. There should only be a desk with a terminal in each one. If you see anything else . . ."

"Shoot," Yanis finished, moving forward.

There was nothing in Jolie's office; she kept her workspace painfully spick-and-span, with the exception of some threads and baubles for the embroidery service that she offered to crew members who wanted to customize their uniforms. Asher's office was also clear; he spent most of his off-duty time volunteering in the nurseries.

When they approached the bulkhead leading to Jacklyn's space, Watson shot an arm across her chest, nearly clotheslining her.

"Jack," Watson warned. "There's an anomaly in your office."

Jacklyn's bruised heart started to beat overtime. "Yanis—"

"Understood," he cut her off, gesturing for two members to flank him as he got in position against the wall. He counted down on his fingers and the team burst around the corner, aiming their guns.

Jacklyn could tell from their reactions that there was nothing there. "Are you sure—" she started to ask Watson.

A bang shook the wall next to her.

Jacklyn spun around so fast she lost her grip on her weapon. She tried frantically to get her finger back on the trigger, feeling the helpless, stretched time that she felt in bad dreams. Long before she recovered, the nearest team member snapped their gun up and blasted the wall.

The fired plasma bolt melted the wall on contact with a concussive burst that made Jacklyn's ears pop even through the suit. The edges of the wound in the metal panel curled back like rotting rind, glowing orange at the tips and releasing faint smoke.

The team flanked the new hole and risked a glance inside. Nobody knew exactly what they were looking for, but it seemed fair to expect some kind of blood splatter or melted flesh inside. The officer closest to the hole shook their head. The blast hadn't hit anything.

"Every shot gives away our position," Yanis growled at Watson. "Mistakes cost lives."

"I didn't make a mistake," Watson retorted. It was the first time Jacklyn had seen the droid get testy. "Something is in the wall."

Jacklyn stepped forward for a look. It was pitch black on the inside since the bulkhead interiors weren't lit. For a moment she thought it was empty as well. Then the headlight in her helmet brushed over something and tossed its shadow on the inner wall.

Careful not to singe or puncture her suit on the edges of the hole, she reached inside. Part of her expected a vicious creature to suddenly snap her arm off in its jaw, or yank her hungrily into the crawl space. Instead her fingers brushed the edge of something almost firm, with enough give to make her think for a horrified moment that she was touching flesh. Just before she jerked her hand back, she realized what it might actually be.

Disgusted, she pulled it out into the open. It was heavy; she had to cradle it in the crook of her elbow. The rest of the team, despite the professionalism they had shown so far, recoiled.

"What the hell is that?" Yanis breathed.

Jacklyn hadn't spent any significant time in the terrariums, nor had she had any entomological training. But she had seen pictures of Earth insects before, and she was fairly certain she recognized the nacre-colored, semi-translucent globule taking up most of her forearm.

"I think it's an egg," she said grimly.

※

The team took a vote.

Yanis and another officer voted to destroy the egg. Nobody knew anything about xenobiology, or what species they had on their hands, or what its life cycle might be. The egg could hatch in the next few minutes; it could be a predator right from birth. Better to smash it now while it was vulnerable before it grew into another murderous intruder.

Jacklyn and the rest of the team voted to bring the egg down to the biologists. This was a live specimen from another world; it needed study for both historic and urgent, practical reasons. Perhaps the bio team could find a way to destroy its mature counterpart.

"We don't have room to bring this along," Yanis argued.

Jacklyn handed the egg to Watson, who cradled it helpfully to its chest. "There we go."

"Fine," Yanis acquiesced, leading them back to the office doors. He took out a bolt of luminescent tape and marked the doorway as cleared. "Just make sure the droid keeps up."

They proceeded to the mission commander's office. Clearing the small room and marking its door was simple. Astronautics and Avionics, on the other hand, took much longer. The departments flashed with lights from star charts and ship schematics, a kaleidoscope that threw deceiving silhouettes and shapes against the walls. More than once Jacklyn saw something in the corner of her eye and turned expecting to be disemboweled, only to find herself looking at a hologram or a reel of old footage from Earth.

Once they cleared the departments, they went back to the corridor. One of the team members hacked into the wall panel for environmental controls and flipped all the level's ventilation and reclamation vents shut. With that, the control deck was completely cut off to anything without the access code to open it back up.

They took a lift down to the tactics deck and covered their tracks by closing off the shaft overhead. The cab couldn't rise to that level anymore; only the captain or mates could reverse the lock.

The first two decks of the *Calypso* were completely isolated from the rest of the ship. They were slowly reducing the creature's roaming area. Eventually they would cut it off with nowhere to go.

The tactics deck was immediately unsettling—every corridor light was off. Yanis took the risk of ordering everyone to increase the brightness on their helmet flashlights, sacrificing the cover of darkness. If the intruder was getting around in the walls, it might already have the advantage of not needing light to see at all.

The tactics deck was nearly double the size of the previous one. Archives, Comms, Systems, Sensors, and Data all had departments on this level. Jacklyn was already intimidated.

"Watson?" She turned toward the droid.

It was making a sling for the egg out of the top of its jumpsuit in order to free its arms. Most droids went without clothing since none of the rest had Watson's anthropomorphic features—it was unique in that it wore a uniform like the rest of the crew. Jacklyn sucked in a breath when she saw that the droid had been given skin all the way down its waist, along with a pair of tiny, lifelike breasts.

Suddenly Watson's increasingly stricken faces in Otto's presence made more sense. Jacklyn felt such disgust in that moment that she could have punched him again.

No one else on the team had any reaction toward the droid. They were focused on approaching the Systems office. It was already sealed, which meant there were crew members inside. Yanis pressed the panel beside the door to ring them.

"Yes?" a techie within answered cautiously.

"This is Senior Security Officer Yanis Kokkinos," Yanis said, his suit venting his voice through a speaker. "Confirm, is your department sealed, including vents and doors?"

"Yes, sir," the techie said with more confidence. The panel changed to show them that the department was completely contained as ordered.

"Carry on until lockdown orders are revoked," Yanis said, satisfied.

"Aye, aye," the techie said, before the line went dead.

They did the same with the Comms and Sensors departments, slapping more luminescent tape along the doorways as they went. Some of the anxiety tightening Jacklyn's shoulders released at the smooth way they moved through this deck. She kept her ears peeled for any ominous banging but heard nothing; every time she glanced back at Watson, the droid gave a negative on any sightings.

Archives wasn't a manned office. The room was full of tall towers of data storage units, each one breathing heavily as the heat-sink paste lathered on the components struggled to keep up with the continual addition of more information.

The team entered in the same order they'd perfected on the previous level, except for Watson.

The droid took one step into the room and immediately backed out. Jacklyn frowned, quickly checking it and the egg for any harm. "What's wrong?"

"It's too loud in there," Watson said apologetically.

The data towers were noiseless to Jacklyn's ears, but she supposed if she could detect every signal passing back and forth between them, she would be overwhelmed too.

Although there were no indications that the intruder held any interest in droids, Jacklyn didn't like leaving it out there by itself. They would have to be quick.

"Wait here," she ordered. "Call me if something happens."

The Archives tower rows were deep, going back far enough that the ends were shrouded in total shadow. Jacklyn's nerves made her see things peeking from the towers and leaning out into the lanes just ahead of the team. Whenever she shone her flashlight on them, however, they disappeared. She walked with one hand ready on her weapon this time.

"Yanis," one of the team members said urgently. "Perseus side, aft."

The rest of the team converged on those directions. Jacklyn knew from the officer's grim but calm voice that it couldn't be an intruder encounter, but her pulse was still rapid as she trailed them to a dim corner with a dark stain on the ground.

In the middle of it was a severed hand.

Jacklyn spun right back around, shuddering at the sight of cracked bone sticking out of mangled red meat where the hand had been torn off. She could hear someone else on the team taking shaky breaths as they examined the scene.

"Not enough blood," they volunteered. "Hand wasn't taken off here."

Jacklyn had seen the mess the intruder left of Panio; this was practically tidy. The blood stain was tacky but not old; whatever had deposited the hand here had done so not that long ago.

Smears of red led away from the corner, even farther back through the data towers. They traded positions methodically as they followed the trail toward the rear of the Archives. Jacklyn was glad for Yanis's clear hand signals because she couldn't hear anything over the rush of her own blood.

The smears stopped right under a vent. Two team members went to either side while the rest knelt and fixed their weapons on the opening. At Yanis's countdown they pried off the vent's grate and flung their weapons inside.

There was no movement or noise in the ventilation shaft. One of the team members quickly darted their helmet inside, but when nothing swiped at them they looked leisurely in both directions and pulled back with confirmation that it was empty yet again.

"Let's clear this deck and shut it down," Yanis said. "If it's still here, we can trap it. If not, we're not letting it come back for its snack."

Right as they turned around to leave, Watson's voice came crackling through their headsets.

"Jack!" it shouted. "Come quick—Data—"

Jacklyn broke into a sprint with the team not far behind her. She nearly burst into the last department on this deck, but

Yanis grabbed the back of her suit and tossed her to the side in the nick of time. He didn't waste his breath berating her—he just signaled for the team to enter in their practiced file.

The doors weren't sealed; they opened on an utterly unfamiliar scene. The department that had been so active and buzzing just a few days ago was empty. The oppressive heat that usually lay over the hive was missing; it felt ominously cold without it.

The workstations were undisturbed. There was no carnage here—no corpses, no missing limbs, no broken bodies. For a moment Jacklyn wondered what the fuss was about, until she saw Watson standing in front of the head data technician's office. When she came to the droid's side, she saw why.

Otto Watson was slumped in his seat with his half-eaten guts spilling out of his lap. The spread of his blood had shorted some of the wires dangling from his terminals. His glasses were askew, eyes staring straight ahead like he was still reading the data flashing on his monitors.

Jacklyn closed her eyes. "He must have come down to do more work against protocol," she muttered. She barely had any nausea left to react with. "Goddamn it."

Yanis and the team closed in to investigate the body. "Fits the CMO's description of the last body," one of them mentioned. "The creature got to him too."

Another officer pointed at Otto's desk. "Here's the rest of that arm."

One of Otto's long, thin arms was stretched out across the desk; where his hand should have been there was only a stump of bloody and ruined meat. The team scanned the office, but there was no evidence that the intruder was still around. From the looks of it, it had snacked on Otto and then left the tactics deck entirely.

"Let's move," Yanis called. "We need to stay ahead of this thing before it catches any more stupid bastards."

Jacklyn was about to follow them out when she noticed something beside the end of Otto's arm. It stood out from the rest of the circuitry and equipment scattered across his desk by virtue of its stark blue cover, the same color as the glow of Watson's eyes. It was a small input chip, the kind that was made to fit inside both terminals and droids. She picked it up and saw that it came with a note:

Give this to Watson. She can still get us home.

Of course the last thing he had been working on was that damn project. If he had just listened to her, if he hadn't been so grossly obsessed with his pet droid, maybe he would still be alive.

She pocketed the chip. She could think about what to do with it—whether she would fulfill his last request—when they weren't in danger.

She left the office to follow the team to the lift but noticed that Watson hadn't budged. It was still in the doorway, staring at Otto's corpse, its expression so complicated that Jacklyn didn't recognize the emotion there, whatever its programming was trying to convey.

"I left him here," Watson confided. "Data was done reconfiguring their systems, so the technicians left for their bunks when you gave the quarantine order—everyone except for the doctor. He was so engrossed in his work that he didn't notice when I sprang the restraints and snuck out."

"The restraints?" Jacklyn echoed sharply.

"He didn't like getting reprimanded," Watson explained. "He wanted an apology for getting him in trouble."

Once again Jacklyn felt sick to her stomach. She had been tempted to feel a little grief at the sight of Otto ripped up and bled out, by virtue of the fact that they shared a home ward, that he had voiced his support when the back-lash of her promotion to first mate hit. But none of that mattered as she watched Watson stare at his inglorious grave.

"It wasn't your fault," she said hotly.

Watson seemed to consider that before confessing, "I'm not sorry for him."

As an officer, Jacklyn wasn't sure how to feel about that, considering the empathy-analog protocol built into every droid system was part of what kept the ship safe from a droid insurrection. As a person, however, she understood. "He used you," she said. "In ways that he never should have. You're allowed to feel that way."

In the dark, Watson's eyes were luminous and eerie as the full moon Jacklyn had seen in pictures. "The Centauri gave him what he deserved."

Jacklyn's skin erupted with gooseflesh at the gentle men-ace in Watson's tone. At the name it gave the intruder. She had nothing to say to that, not while they still had a job to do. "Come on."

They jogged to catch up with everyone at the lift, where Yanis gave them both a hard look. Jacklyn asked with her eyes for him to drop it. He let her know with his that this was a one-time courtesy, before closing all the vents on the deck and marking it done.

＊

They left the corpse. There wasn't time to bring Otto down to the morgue; he would have to remain at his desk until they eliminated his killer. For now they continued clearing the bow so they could rendezvous with the other teams.

They entered the labs deck near the astrophysics laboratory, where Jacklyn had done maintenance work. It was quiet and dark, and the memory of the banging was sinister in her mind. She kept her ears peeled, but the corridor was quiet all the way down.

This deck had been little used recently, so clearing the laboratories went quickly. They marked doorframes at a good pace. Still, Jacklyn felt her skin crawl with a nameless dread. She kept one eye on Watson at all times, waiting for the droid to announce another anomaly.

Eventually they entered the part of the deck under the most intense repairs. They avoided where the scaffolding was barely holding; those locations were already sealed, exposed as they were to the void. Instead, the team went into the last lab, barely intact.

Jacklyn felt more unsettled here than in any other room they had cleared so far. The lab looked like the ones that she had seen in old, two-dimensional movies: crowded with esoteric apparatuses, chemical cabinets, and strange vats and flasks. Instead of the bright white light sterilizing those scenes, however, this part of the deck was shadowy. The team had to move carefully through the abandoned equipment; a single wrong step would send the paused experiments crashing down around them.

In the middle of their careful prowl, they heard glass shatter.

Yanis spun to shoot an accusatory look at the team, but when everyone glanced at their steps and checked that they had disturbed nothing, he swung back around with his weapon drawn. Jacklyn's adrenaline spiked as he motioned them forward, hands sweaty in the gloves of her suit.

They were heading toward the back of the lab when they heard a scream.

It was shrill and agonized, the kind of scream that shredded vocal cords. The kind of scream that had come from Panio as he was ripped apart. The team broke into a controlled sprint, going after the sound.

As they ran, however, Watson's voice broke through their headsets.

"I sense no one here," the droid said, confused.

Yanis didn't stop their advance as he barked, "What?"

"Infrared sensors aren't reading anything," Watson clarified. "Neither are motion detectors."

Yanis stopped the team at the end of the laboratory where the breach seal was. This was the darkest part of the lab—the lights had popped when the lab was exposed to vacuum. Earth-normal conditions evaporated here, where the engineers reduced pressure differentials for their work. It was hard to see anything around the corner where they were posted. Yanis did another countdown, and two officers swung their weapons into the open.

One of them gasped as their lights illuminated the body

on the floor. Instead of messy carnage though, this one was picked clean. Its organs had been eaten away so that its pried-open rib cage and spine were visible. The blood on the floor was dark, crusted brown.

This body was very old.

One of the team members shouldered their weapon. "We all heard a scream, right?"

"Didn't come from this lady," another member answered, bending for a closer look at the missing viscera.

Jacklyn turned around to ask Watson what it could sense, but movement behind the officer bringing up the team's rear caught her attention. She only had time to suck in a breath before a shadow fell upon him.

She screamed right as he did.

It was impossible to see what happened next. The shadow cinched around the officer hard enough to puncture his suit and the skin beneath, making his blood burst out in a spray, powered by the outgassing of the air trapped in his lungs and guts. Red flecked Jacklyn's helmet; she stumbled back so fast that she tripped over a piece of debris. Her headlight detached from her suit and rolled on the ground, creating a strobe effect as the other team members brought up their weapons and fired.

Jacklyn scrambled to retrieve her light and get back on her feet. The thunder of plasma shots disoriented her; she ducked her head as she tried to reattach her light with shaking hands.

Suddenly Watson was kneeling in front of her, doing the work with precise, mechanical motions and pulling her one-handed back to her feet. Jacklyn patted her waist for her weapon and swung it up just as the firefight stopped.

The circle of the team's collective light revealed the body on the ground. The officer wasn't moving; Jacklyn could see his helmet was cracked, leaving his face swollen and iced over with crystals of what used to be his breath. Nobody dared to help him, not with the bigger shadow lying just outside the illumination.

Jacklyn couldn't see the creature clearly, but she could make out its size. It was massive, even sprawled across the ground, sizzling with the heat of several plasma shots in what seemed to be its side. She squinted, trying to identify more of its features in the dark, but she was shaken by the sound of another shrill scream.

It was the same agonized screech from before, like someone was being killed right next to them. But Jacklyn knew better now—that sound wasn't human.

Before the team could converge on the downed creature, another shadow reared up from the darkness. The sound of flesh dragging against metal filled the lab as a second creature pulled the dead one out of sight.

"Engage!" Yanis shouted. The team lurched into pursuit.

This time they didn't care how much noise or destruction they made; they bulldozed through the lab, dashing equipment to the floor. Jacklyn scrubbed at the blood on her helmet as she ran, her pulse thundering in her veins. She was relieved to hear the heavy thunk of Watson running right behind her.

Their pursuit took them all the way out of the lab. In the lights of the corridor they could see smears of strange, bright blue blood. The tracks led all the way to a vent with its grate pried off.

The creatures had escaped.

"Damn it!" Yanis shouted, banging his hand on the

bulkhead. The other officers dropped their weapons, shell-shocked.

Jacklyn felt the same. Her eyes were fixed on the splotches of alien blood, almost the same shade as the Terran oceans that every child was shown in their nursery. The color was oddly, impossibly beautiful. A wave of reassurance swept over Jacklyn that the creatures could be wounded by the crew's weapons, but a strange, fey part of her stared admiringly at the vibrant stains.

The security team recovered their composure. Jacklyn woke from her trance to Yanis waving permission to a few officers, his face dark and tight like a fist. Those team members broke off and reentered the lab.

"Jack," Watson said, drawing her attention. The droid knelt beside her and tore a piece of fabric from its uniform top, swiping it through some of the creature's blood. It wasn't thin like human blood but viscous, almost a slime. Watson folded the sample thoughtfully into the cloth before tucking it in with the egg. "We have one more deck to go."

Jacklyn shook off her fog. They had made contact with the creature, a real, undeniable lifeform unlike anything she had been taught about from Earth. They had seen for themselves its carnage, and how dangerous it could be in an instant. It was her responsibility to make sure the rest of the ship didn't suffer the same fate.

"All teams, this is Jack from delta team," she announced through her headset, broadcasting to everyone on the hunt. "Contact confirmed. Beware: there are multiple intruders onboard."

7

They had to leave the fallen officer behind.

Just as there had been no time to move Otto's body from its pool of blood and gore, they had no time to move the officer from the laboratory. Jacklyn could hear the team members who went back closing his suit as best as they could and straightening his horribly sprawled limbs. She might have heard stifled crying as well, but it didn't last long.

The officers returned without further dallying, sidestepping the blue blood on the ground, and the whole team fell back to the lift. Yanis quickly shut the vents and sealed the level as they descended to the final deck in the bow.

Clearing the observation deck was simple. The whole level was open to the stars, with little blocking the panorama of interstellar space; the only fixtures were the viewing benches and the information consoles in the center of its atrium. The team split into two groups, walking the room's giant circumference in opposite directions. They met up without incident on the other side. Jacklyn only stopped once to look out the window by habit. She was too frazzled to find the Sun among the constellations; the stars looked like random stitches, a nonsensical embroidery she had no time to untangle.

They sealed the deck with a sense of finality, ensuring the front of the *Calypso* was closed off for good. Then they took a lift all the way down to Sickbay.

Yanis kept his weapon drawn the whole ride while two

officers kept eyes on the ceiling hatch. Jacklyn half expected the lift to shake again with the weight of another creature tilting the cab, making it shriek and grind along the shaft. She didn't know if the lift could handle that with the whole team inside; maybe she wouldn't die from being torn apart but from plummeting to her death in false grav instead. She didn't know which one would be messier.

When the doors opened, every officer pointed their weapon into the corridor. Although it was empty, nobody let their guard down. They proceeded in formation all the way to the sealed Sickbay doors. The team angled themselves outward protectively while Yanis and Jacklyn sent a message through the door panel.

"Wang," Jacklyn called. "It's us."

"With another sample delivery," Yanis added.

A group of medical officers let them through. They stared, horrified, as the team entered with their blood-spattered suits, and wasted no time sealing the doors after them.

No one on this deck was wearing the protective gear that the other sealed decks necessitated, since Sickbay was structurally removed from the rest of the ship. It had its own ventilation and reclamation systems. The only things connecting it to the other decks were the lift shafts. It was the safest place on the ship.

The team took the opportunity to ditch their helmets. Jacklyn shivered as cool air blew across her sweaty skin, humid from her heavy breathing; she had been panting too much for the suit's equilibrium system to keep up. She was glad to get the blood spray out of her view.

There was no time to rest, however. She and Watson went

to the temporary bio lab. They found the researchers bent over several datapads, marveling over the results from the earlier excrement sample.

"If you liked that," Jacklyn quipped without humor, "you're going to love this."

The bio team erupted into exclamations as Watson unwrapped the egg. Someone wheeled over a new gurney at light speed, and they switched out their equipment for sterile gear as they took the egg and cut off the blood-soaked part of Watson's uniform for analysis. As soon as the droid was relieved of its package, Jacklyn pulled it to the side and slipped the tunic of some stolen scrubs over its head, covering its bare, blue-smeared breasts.

She was surprised when the droid gave her a wide smile. "Thank you, Jack."

The heartbreakingly familiar look lanced through Jacklyn like sharp claws. Unlike the times when she had looked at the droid's face and felt only grief, this smile pulled one out of her too.

She turned back to the researchers, gesturing toward the egg. "Can you get something useful out of that?"

The head techie gave her an incredulous look. "Yes, Jack, I think we can get something useful out of this novel astrobiological specimen."

"Don't get smart," Jacklyn growled. "Let me know if you can find a weakness, anything we can use to exterminate the creatures."

"I'll see what we can do," the techie promised apologetically, already turning back to the sample.

With her team's objective accomplished and their payload

successfully delivered, Jacklyn's adrenaline seeped away. The toll of the horror and pursuit hit her like a pipe to the head. She found herself swaying on her feet.

Watson appeared beside her. "Are you okay?"

Jacklyn slapped her hands hard against her cheeks. "I'll be fine," she said for her own benefit. She couldn't sleep just yet; there was still work to be done.

She went to the CMO's office. "Hey," she said, gently pulling Wang from the pitiful nap he was taking folded at his desk. "How come you aren't freaking out over the alien we brought you?"

"Did that." Wang yawned. "But my specialty is Earth biology. Couldn't keep up. What do you need?"

Jacklyn was going to keel over in a second. "Stimulant?"

Wang's exhausted look collapsed into severe displeasure. "Jack, when's the last time you slept?"

Jacklyn didn't appreciate the question. "The ship's still not safe. There are creatures out there murdering our crew. We lost one of our own just now. I can sleep after this is over."

Wang grumbled as he retrieved the shot, sticking her none too gently with the depressor. The effect was nearly immediate; Jacklyn's wooziness cleared like gas blown back by a star. With the boost of energy, she went to check in with the other teams.

She walked up to Yanis, who was downing a packet of nutrigel. "Roll call?" she suggested.

He borrowed a pad from a med techie and opened a channel to the other security teams still clearing their regions of the ship.

"Theta team, come in," he ordered.

After a moment the theta team leader answered. "Delta

team, we're here. Finishing up our sector now. No contact or sightings." They were responsible for the uppermost decks of the wards.

"Kappa team?" Yanis called, switching channels.

That team responded in the affirmative, as did lambda team, sigma team, and all the rest responsible for ward decks. The going was slow since those were the widest and largest parts of the ship. Those teams had to pause and check that all the bunks were secure, with no hotshots trying to roam against orders. Jacklyn was heartened to hear that besides one episode of loud banging, there were no signs of the creatures in the populated decks.

"The last two teams?" Jacklyn asked.

Psi team was responsible for the hold and Life Support, while omega team was on Engineering. It was a tall job. The top end of the stern was packed with maintenance offices, machine shops, and more. At the extreme end of the ship was the engine interface and energy core. Some of those decks required extremophile suits to enter due to temperature and radiation levels, and conditions on the last few would obliterate any organics; those wouldn't need clearing. That still left a lot of ground to cover.

There were several harrowing minutes during which no one answered Yanis's call. Psi team finally reported in—with the worst news.

"Delta team." Their leader was barely audible; there was major interference on their line. "We've engaged the intruder . . . lost three team members. Creature got away . . . no contact with omega . . ."

Jacklyn felt ill. Michiko had gone with omega team, since their assignment was so demanding. She would never miss a check-in during an emergency like this. Jacklyn knew what the radio silence meant.

Yanis jerked, surprised, when Jacklyn grabbed her discarded weapon and fastened her helmet again. "You're going back out there?"

"You heard them—something's wrong." Her ears popped as her suit sealed again. She yanked a cloth from a nearby medical cabinet and swiped the blood from the glass in front of her face. "We cleared the bow, and it sounds like the wards are good too. That means the creatures are in the stern."

Watson came to stand beside her. "I can't find omega team—something is interfering with feeds and comms."

Jacklyn's resolve hardened. "I'm leaving now."

Yanis snorted. "Who do you think you're going to save by yourself? You're a terrible shot."

Jacklyn accepted the chastisement, half because it was true and half because he was already fastening his suit as well. "I still have to try."

"Damn it, Jack," one of the team members sighed, grabbing their helmet. "You're making us look bad."

"I'm not getting shown up by bridge crew," another declared hotly.

Within a minute the entire team was ready to go. They were all bloodstained and pale with exhaustion. The creases on their faces belied their cheekiness—they understood what they were volunteering for. It was obvious in their reduced number.

Jacklyn felt like she should make a speech, but she couldn't find any words and her stimulant would only last for so much longer. This was the last time she would feel safe—quite possibly ever.

"Let's go."

※

The lift doors opened

None of the reserve lights in Engineering were on. The icy anxiety that had melted off of Jacklyn during their stop in Sickbay prickled her skin once again as the team stepped onto the deck, their lights swinging back and forth. The illumination only reached a few feet before the darkness snuffed it out. That was more than close enough for one of the creatures to jump out at them before they could get their weapons up.

Yanis took a breath that shuddered down their line before gesturing them forward.

As they passed stations and storage units, they saw many doorways already marked with luminescent tape, showing omega team's progress. The engineers' office also had a mark. Jacklyn gestured for Yanis to let her approach. The team huddled up, watching her back.

"Watson, is anyone in there?" Jacklyn asked urgently.

"There are several crew present," Watson said right away, "including the first and second engineers."

Jacklyn tapped the door panel. "Viktorija, Kachi. It's Jack. Report?"

Several moments passed in which Jacklyn wondered if Watson had gotten it wrong, but Viktorija eventually answered. "Jack," she said hoarsely. "You came."

"Are you hurt?" Jacklyn demanded. "Who else is in there? Have you seen the security team that came this way?"

"I'm with my repair crew—we holed up when you gave the order," Viktorija said. "The only one hurt is Kachi. He was bringing up the rear. He's . . . in a bad way." She paused. "The security team is here. The ones we could recover."

The deck started to spin around Jacklyn. She squeezed her eyes shut against the vertigo. ". . . Michiko?"

Viktorija's voice was very soft. "I have her, Jack."

Jacklyn thought she had no more nausea left in her, but she was wrong. She felt like gagging again, this time on the tears tightening her throat.

"We need to get Kachi to Sickbay," Viktorija continued. "He can still be saved."

Jacklyn tried to respond, but speaking threatened to trigger her gullet and let grief spew out.

"Stay put," Yanis ordered, taking over. "We still need to clear the stern."

"Be careful," Viktorija warned. "From what I saw, those beasts are tough. Nothing drops them except the plasma guns. Only high-energy attacks seem to work—something about them makes everything else ping right off. My guess is they have some kind of natural electromagnetic defense."

It was their star, Jacklyn realized. Proxima Centauri was a disgruntled red dwarf, constantly belching out flares due to its own magnetic indigestion. Anything that evolved on the surface of one of its worlds would have to develop their own organic defense to the energy lashings and charged particle rain.

That explained a lot: the overheating droid, the glitching terminals, and Watson's fuzzy blind spots. They were dealing with an apex Centauri predator.

Jacklyn couldn't pinch herself through her suit, so she leaned hard enough against the wall that it made a deep bruise in her hip. The pain cleared her throat. "Got it. We'll come back for you."

"Be careful," Viktorija pleaded again, right before the connection cut out.

This floor of Engineering had already been taped. The

team proceeded carefully through the corridor and then down a set of stairs to the next level, a gun pointed in every direction. Watson's eyes were wide, pushing its sensing capacity to its limits.

They touched down on the floor of the engine interface, a huge chamber stretching from hull to hull, so cavernous that their flashlights couldn't penetrate the darkness to the ceiling or the sides. Enormous pipes coiled back and forth like intestinal tracts between the walls and deck, circulating fusion energy and radioactive waste away from the core. It was a shadowy labyrinth of the ducts, siphons, and cylinders that pumped the ship's veins and kept her running. The interface was the last level of the ship before the propulsion module that sailed them through the cosmic sea.

Jacklyn felt the darkness bearing down on them like an extra atmosphere. Her hindbrain insisted something was waiting for them beyond the pitiful cones of their lights, ready to pounce as soon as they let their guard down. Apparently it wasn't just her imagination.

"I sense them," Watson whispered.

Ice ran down Jacklyn's back. "How many?"

"One," Watson counted. After a moment, it added, "Two." And then, "Three."

Jacklyn hadn't bargained for that. She looked toward Yanis, who immediately beckoned the team behind one of the huge pipes rising out of the floor. They took cover under its mazy twists, one of the officers posted as a lookout.

"We just need to cross the interface to the other lift," Yanis murmured. Jacklyn could hear his breath coming harder too. "Then we can seal this deck and regroup to make a plan. We don't need to take them all out—we just need to trap them here until we can bring reinforcements. Understood?"

"Understood," the team responded. Everyone looked ghostly and drawn in the faint illumination of their helmet lights.

"I want someone on our ass at all times," Yanis said. "Jack, take the middle. Have your droid give us updates on the creatures' positions every ten meters."

"Understood," Jacklyn echoed, her heart beating hard enough to burst. She wondered if she should have skipped the stimulant after all, what with renewed adrenaline making her febrile.

Yanis waited for everyone on the team to take a few deep breaths and fix their grips on their weapons. Then he signaled for them to move forward.

The instant they were beyond the cover of the pipe, Jacklyn felt such an electrifying sense of exposure that she seized, her legs locking her where she stood. Her body tried to skip both fight and flight to settle on freeze—a shove from the officer behind her made her trip back into motion.

They made it to the next enormous pipe without incident, ducking under its makeshift cover. Jacklyn was breathing hard enough to fog her helmet again. She wondered if this was how gazelles used to feel on the Serengeti before it burned, hyperaware of something following them in the grass. She swung her gun back and forth, no longer feeling like the one on the hunt.

"Watson." Her voice came out reedy. "Update?"

"I'm not sure," Watson hedged.

"Droid," Yanis snapped. "We need their positions."

"Deck sensors are jammed again," it replied, peering into the darkness.

The electromagnetic defense, Jacklyn guessed. With Watson blind and deaf they would be easy pickings—they had to do something or else they would all go the same way as Michiko's team.

"Give me a prod." Jacklyn snatched her own off of her belt and took one from the nearest officer. She switched them on and slid both all the way to their maximum settings.

Electricity popped from the ends of the prods. Her suit was insulated, so she wasn't in danger of frying herself, but she could still feel the energy the prods were shedding. Sparks showered down on the metal gratings underfoot.

"I'm gonna make a flare. Look away," she warned the team. "Watson, tell me what you see."

She closed her eyes and touched the prods together.

The arc that lanced between them glowed so bright Jacklyn could see it through her eyelids. It wasn't nearly enough to light the whole room, but it gave Watson's ultrasensitive pupils enough illumination to detect a hulking shadow prowling toward them.

"Three o'clock!" the droid cried shrilly.

Yanis and the other officers swiveled. A round of shots tore blazing holes through the interface's darkness, plasma flashing brilliant white as it blitzed through the air. Jacklyn could hear the sizzle of the shots hitting their mark.

An agonized scream ripped apart the quiet.

"The Centauri is down!" Watson reported.

"Advance!" Yanis bellowed.

Watson grabbed Jacklyn, still blinking away dancing spots, and pulled her forward. The team jogged out of cover, passing through a grid of cargo elevators meant to bring replacement parts to and from the pipes; the wide platforms provided a buffer between them and the open. They paused before making a break for the next set of pipes, looking to Watson for information on their quarry.

"Straight ahead," Watson declared, and then immediately backtracked. "No, ten o'clock."

"You'll get us killed, droid!" Yanis roared, swinging his weapon back and forth. "Which is it?"

"Their movements are erratic," Watson said defensively.

Jacklyn knew the droid was trying its best, which was the only reason she wasn't shouting at it too. She fingered the control of her prod again, but it was shot—her makeshift flare had broken it.

Watson frowned. "I believe the Centauri know they're being tracked."

Jacklyn had thought their situation couldn't get any worse, but clearly she hadn't been thinking hard enough. Watson continued scanning the darkness, glowing eyes swinging this way and that. Suddenly the droid's neck snapped back. "Above!"

Jacklyn flung herself to the side just before a huge dark shape hurtled into their midst, dropping meteorite-fast and crushing one of the team members under its heavy weight. The officer didn't have time to scream—the only sound they made was the crunch of bone and squish of flesh. Quick as Jacklyn could blink, the creature tore into the officer's soft parts, and the radius of their blood splatter flung outward.

The team scattered.

Jacklyn couldn't see where they went—she just tripped into a hard run away from the horrific smacking of meat,

Watson at her heels. The droid wasn't the only thing chasing her—she could hear the metallic shriek of huge, sharp claws galloping across the grated floors.

"To the core!" Yanis yelled.

Though Jacklyn was well acquainted with this level, terror made her disoriented. She didn't know which way to go; all the pipes looked the same. Meanwhile the sounds of the Centauri in hot pursuit got closer and closer.

"This way, Jack!"

Watson grabbed her arm and pulled her down a narrow aisle in the conduits. It was so tight that Jacklyn's helmet banged on the metal to either side as she stumbled through. Eventually the aisle opened into a cavity under the lattice of drains that sent onboard waste to be incinerated in the core. Jacklyn slid into a cleft in the machinery and was jostled by the arrival of the rest of the team.

All of them were panting heavily. Jacklyn was ruining her helmet's visibility again with how hard her panicked breaths were coming. The closest officer grabbed her hand and squeezed it painfully until she stopped hyperventilating.

Jacklyn counted the people in the cavity. There were two team members left. She bit her lip bloody with worry until she glimpsed Yanis sidling down the aisle toward them. Everyone shuffled around in the tight space to let him in.

"We need to make a break for it," he advised.

"They're too fast, sir," one officer protested. "In an all-out sprint they're going to smoke us."

"That's why I'm going to make a distraction," Yanis said gravely. "Get to the other lift and seal the deck while I hold them off."

The other officers immediately launched into objections, but Jacklyn looked closer at Yanis, pale and clammy inside his helmet. He had one hand on his gun and the other pressed to his side; underneath his hand a stain was growing on his suit.

"You're bleeding," Jacklyn said hollowly.

Yanis nodded, lifting his arm so they could see where his suit was punctured. "It got me when it dropped. I won't make it."

The officers looked shaken. "Sir—"

Yanis cut them off. "Take the lanes near the core door—those bastards are too big to follow there. Head back to the office, grab the second engineer, and lock the creatures down here while you hightail it to Sickbay."

The team got ready mechanically. Everyone tried to ignore how Yanis was slowly forming a puddle beneath them. He raised a hand, and they moved into position on his countdown.

It was a tight squeeze in the interwoven bowels of the ship. Yanis led the way, followed by an officer; Jacklyn and Watson tailed them, while the last team member took up the rear. The deck was silent again; intuition told Jacklyn they were being watched.

"They're following us," Watson confirmed quietly. "From above."

Jacklyn shivered and hefted her gun. She didn't look up; her headlight couldn't reach far enough to bring the Centauri into relief, and she wasn't sure she wanted to see what was hunting them anyway.

The tapered lanes in the conduits took them most of the way to the other side of the deck. The team came to a cautious stop right before the pipes ended and the exposed distance to the deck's second staircase began.

"On my mark . . ." Yanis whispered.

Jacklyn gulped. She couldn't see anything, but she knew the creatures were out there. She turned instinctively to Watson, but the droid shook its head; the Centauri were jamming it again. They would just have to take a leap of faith.

"Now!"

They burst outward at full tilt.

As soon as they were in the open, the creatures leaped after them.

The metal grating below groaned under their weight. The noise that their sharp feet—pincers or talons or something unknown—made as they chased them came closer and closer. Jacklyn chanced a single glance backward. She could only see the faintest silhouettes of the creatures, fast and sleek. The way the shadows in the interface rolled over them reminded Jacklyn of panthers from Earth, though these beasts were much more massive. She didn't look anymore as she pumped her legs and picked up the pace.

She only knew that they passed the core door because the sounds of pursuit stalled and Yanis's last scream crackled across the team's connection. She gasped but kept going, aiming for the stairs just outside the cone of her headlight. Right as she reached the railing, Watson grabbed her hard enough to make her shout and yanked her back.

A creature dropped down right on top of where she used to be.

The other officers sprayed a lightning storm of plasma shots. Jacklyn couldn't make out whether they had hit the creature through her light-stung eyes. She didn't stay to find out, following Watson's painful tugging back toward the core.

"There are still three Centauri," it said as they tried to take cover again in the ducts. "Four . . . five . . . !"

"Jesus!" one of the team cried. "How many of these bastards are there?"

"We're not gonna make it," the other panted. "There's no way—!"

Jacklyn felt the hysteria rising and cut through the chatter. "Shut up and run! There can't be that many—only one silo was depleted. Just keep going—"

Someone screamed as they were pulled back into the dark.

The last officer fired their gun behind them and kicked the pace up even more. Jacklyn's lungs were burning; her helmet rang with a warning that she was taking in too much oxygen. She could feel the air getting hotter and hotter closer to the core—there were radiation shields in place, but that didn't stop all of it from leaking out. Her suit could only metabolize so much; she started to sweat even more.

The remnants of the team slammed to a stop at the airlock before the core door. Both Jacklyn and the last officer were shaking like overworked horses; Watson stared into the pitch black behind them.

"They're closing in!" it warned.

The charge on their plasma guns was getting low. Jacklyn ran the numbers and arrived at just one answer. "Get inside!"

The officer stared at her with huge, reddened eyes. "The radiation—"

They didn't have time to debate. Jacklyn smashed the panel next to the airlock handle and forced it open. "I said get in!"

The officer hesitated a second too long—before Jacklyn could seize them and toss them inside, something reached down from the pipe above and snatched them screaming into the air.

Watson spun around and gave her a mighty push. It knocked the wind out of her and sent her sailing through the door, which the droid slammed shut behind her. When Jacklyn shook off her daze and sprang back up, she found herself inside the airlock alone. The droid was out there with the Centauri.

"Watson!" she yelled. "What the hell are you doing?"

"I'm helping, Jack," it replied. "Stay there and I will—"

Watson's voice cut out in Jacklyn's helmet right as she heard a loud crunch beyond the thick door. There was the deafening bang of metal on metal and then nothing at all.

"Watson," Jacklyn whispered. "Watson."

The only response was a broken crackle across the line.

Jacklyn tried to think of what to do. She couldn't stay in the airlock indefinitely—temperatures were quickly becoming uncomfortable and the radiation poisoning the officer had feared would become a reality if she didn't find a safe way out. Her plan had been to stall in here while Watson sent a message to the other teams.

She tried to think of another plan, but she was close to boiling in her suit and her mind couldn't focus on anything other than the horrible sound she'd heard before Watson went silent. If the Centauri had harmed the droid—

The handle to the airlock moved.

Her breathing ratcheted again. Something was opening the door from the other side. The short, jerky progress of the handle told her that it wasn't Watson.

She groped for her gun—at this distance, she could surely make a direct hit. She realized with dawning horror, however, that her weapon wasn't on her; it must have fallen when Watson shoved her inside. Terrified, she looked around the airlock for something she could use, anything.

It was just her and the final door to the core.

Jacklyn stared at it. It was the thickest door on the ship, assembled during the *Calypso*'s construction with even more care than the glass windows that separated the crew from the void. Right behind the door was an energy lattice keeping most of the core's immense power from spilling out into the engineering deck; still, opening it would release a flood of radiation so intense it could make her skin slough off and her guts fall out in mere minutes.

Behind her, the airlock swung open.

Jacklyn lunged for the core, typing her input at light speed and waiting for the authorization to take effect. She heard the whoosh of something like claws hook into the air where she had just stood, and slammed herself against the farthest wall while the core slowly unlocked. Tucked into the corner, she got her first glimpse of the thing that had taken so many of her people.

Most of the creature was hidden behind the airlock door; it was too big to fit across the threshold. Instead it swiped at her through the opening with a limb that ended in the razor heels that had cut open Vidal, Panio, and so many more.

Jacklyn was shaking so badly her headlight couldn't illuminate more than that. The only other thing she could make out was the hardened sheen of the creature's flesh, a jet black that shimmered iridescent like the carapace of a beetle. She had the feverish thought that it suited the Centauri, a fitting shell for a home world with a sun that destroyed rather than nurtured.

The core chimed and swung open.

Jacklyn only left it ajar for a split second. She was behind the heavy-duty door, shielded from the arc of energy that burst out of the opening with the violence of a solar flare. That split second was enough—instead of a flash from a ruddy dwarf like Proxima Centauri, it was a burst from a blazing yellow star like the Sun.

The creature screeched, shrill and agonized, as the energy from the core burned it alive. Its carapace started to bubble and crack; steam rose from the seams in its limbs as it cooked inside its shell.

Jacklyn watched for a horrified moment. Then she cut off the radiation by shoving the door shut.

Everything went dark again. Jacklyn's eyesight was ruined from the blaze of light, but she could feel the tremble in the floor as the creature hit the deck, dead in its skin.

Half-blind, she stumbled outside the airlock, sidestepping the smoking lump on the ground. By squinting she could see Watson's tiny, crumpled body slumped against the wall. The false skin of its arms was ruined again, melted to a puddle by its sides. Its chassis was completely crushed. Jacklyn's knees gave out; she crawled over as quickly as she could.

For a moment she wondered if she had killed it too. "Watson?"

The blue glow returned to Watson's eyes as the droid revived. "Jack," it said, but instead of the smooth tones that

Otto had designed, the word was staticky, like a twentieth-century radio.

Jacklyn didn't care—she threw her arms around the droid, small enough that it disappeared into her hug. "You saved me."

"My pleasure," Watson insisted, glitchy.

Jacklyn pulled back. "I killed one of the creatures. Where are the others?"

Watson's expression grew distant as it checked. With all the damage to its body, Jacklyn could hear it whirring as it worked like a regular old terminal.

"They're gone," it announced. "The Centauri are no longer in the interface. I believe they've retreated to the walls."

Jacklyn couldn't afford to relax at the news. "I have to seal the deck while they're gone. Can you walk?"

Watson struggled to its feet. Its chest was caved in from a great blow, like the creature from before had knocked it harshly aside. Jacklyn could see through the ruined scrubs that its breasts had been destroyed; she felt a grim satisfaction on its behalf. The rest of the droid seemed to be in working order, so they went as quickly as they could across the deck and up the other stairs.

The people holed up in the engineers' office opened the door at Jacklyn's call. Their suits were covered in blood like hers, but they seemed unharmed with the exception of On-yekachi, who had a nasty wound stretching down his back from his shoulder to his hip. Viktorija carried him and led the engineers to the unsealed lift. Jacklyn stood by with her hands on her recovered weapon while they filed out.

She glanced into the dimly lit office when it finally emptied out. Arranged in neat, respectful rows on the floor were the bodies of omega team. She had to blink away the sting in her eyes when they fell on Michiko, looking just as authoritative as she had in life even with some of her limbs missing below the joints.

"Jack," Viktorija called down the corridor. The repair team was cramped around her in the lift. "Are you coming?"

"Go ahead," Jacklyn said, gesturing at the tight fit. "I'll be right there."

Viktorija looked like she wanted to argue. Since Onyekachi didn't have much time, she simply nodded and pressed the button for Sickbay. The lift doors closed and left Jacklyn and Watson alone on the deck.

Jacklyn leaned against the wall, using it to stay upright. Whatever boost she'd had from Wang's stimulant was gone. She fought off sleep and asked, "Creatures?"

"Still none," Watson reassured her.

She went to the environmental controls and dutifully sealed the vents, marking off the level with the last of delta team's luminescent tape. The security teams had fulfilled their priorities: they had gotten the Centauri away from the crew and narrowed down the places they could be on the ship. Once the teams regrouped, they could isolate their location and get rid of the rest once and for all.

"We did it," Watson said, grinning. Its faceplate was shattered on one side and scorched on the other, but that didn't matter—its smile was no less bright than the one Kimberly used to shine at Jacklyn, the kind that made her think of solid ground and water that stretched across the horizon.

"We did it," she agreed. She held out a fist the way she always used to, and felt something bittersweet as Watson reverently tapped her knuckles with its own.

"We should rendezvous with the others," Watson advised as the lift returned to Engineering. They climbed into the cab. "All the decks are cleared now."

"Yeah—" Jacklyn was about to press the button for Sickbay, when a horrifying realization froze her hand in midair. "Shit," she whispered, and then slammed her hand on the lift wall. "Shit!"

The security teams had cleared every deck—except one.

8

The lift stopped on the command quarters deck.

The whole ride up Jacklyn trembled with the expectation that the ceiling hatch would be pried apart by alien talons, and she would paint the walls of the lift red. She had to unlock and relock every deck that they passed, making sure that the Centauri couldn't follow them up the shaft. They had forgotten this deck in the chaos of being attacked; she went down the corridor with her gun drawn, the only armed member of her team left.

"Dad!" she called at the captain's bunk. She tried the panel on the bulkhead; when that went unanswered, she pummeled the door. "Are you in there?"

That damned silence again. For the past week it had needled Jacklyn, taunting her with the knowledge that the man she admired—the man who commanded the respect of a six-thousand-strong crew, who kept not just the peace but also the prosperity of a ship on a mission fated for failure— had abandoned his duties without a single word as to why.

Now instead of anger the silence made her eyes burn with dismay.

Jacklyn turned to Watson. "Can you see him?"

The droid stared at the wall separating them from the captain's quarters. "I can see officers sealed and suited up in all cabins, except this one. Motion detectors are reporting something in the captain's bunk, but I don't know what it is."

Jacklyn felt her stomach roil. She clenched her hand on her weapon. "Dad?"

Sensors on the fritz were a bad sign. Could they have been tampered with? Or were they experiencing that peculiar electromagnetic defense? Maybe the Centauri hadn't been trapped down in Engineering after all—

Jacklyn jumped when a bang shook the door from the other side.

"Watson," she hissed, stepping in front of the droid. She aimed at the bunk, finger on the trigger. "Get back."

The door unlocked with a click. Jacklyn's heart was going fast enough to make it back to Earth tomorrow. She had one chance to make a direct hit; the price for missing was her guts, and maybe even the rest of Watson's parts. She couldn't let that happen.

The door opened. Her finger twitched.

"Wait!" Watson cried.

Nothing leaped out at them. There was no black, hulking mass behind the threshold. The only thing Jacklyn could see through the doorway was a tall, disheveled figure.

Her father.

He was propped unsteadily on the edge of his bunk. His locs, which had hung thick, dark, and beautiful down his back all her life, had been picked apart at the ends. The salt-and-pepper beard that he kept close to his jaw had begun to curl up his cheeks. His brows were drawn down over wide-blown eyes, with pupils so dilated they looked like binary black holes.

"Jack," her father greeted her for the first time in a week.

Jacklyn stared. There were shriveled nutrigel packets littering the bunk. A rank stench wafted out of his empty, overturned terminal monitor. Clothes and bedding were heaped on the floor in an unwashed nest. It looked nothing like the tidy space he had taught her to make of all her accommodations, nothing like the cozy, inviting room she and her sister used to pile inside for nights when they watched Earth recordings together.

Jacklyn had expected to feel some kind of relief at the sight of him alive and whole, but the feeling that glowed white-hot in her chest was fury.

"So you *were* in there," she whispered. "This whole time. Ignoring the calls, shirking your duty. Listening to everyone else die."

She expected some kind of apology, or at least some bull-shit explanation. Instead, he gave her a small smile.

"Your mother was right, you know," Noah said. His voice was hoarse from reclusion, and his tone was strange.

The hairs on Jacklyn's nape stood up. "What do you mean?" she asked lowly, even though she already knew.

"She used to beg me to make the ship go faster," he sighed, pulling himself to his feet. "She said the ship was infested, and the longer we took to reach home the worse the vermin would get."

Jacklyn had so many memories of her mother ranting and raving. Tegan had tried to tell them. "How did she figure it out?"

"She heard things in the walls," her father explained, making Jacklyn's breath catch. "Then she found out she wasn't the only one. She gathered other crew members who heard them too."

Jacklyn had never known how Tegan managed to assemble the people in her cult, loyal followers who injected themselves with the same stolen depressors from Sickbay as she had.

"As quartermaster she had access to stats about our stores," Noah continued. He took a mincing step forward, like his legs were asleep. Jacklyn instinctively stepped back. "The numbers convinced her she was right. She radioed other quartermasters in the flotilla—they reported similar discrepancies."

"Why didn't they send the stats to the fleet?" Jacklyn demanded.

"Tegan was convinced it was something we picked up on Proxima b, something the colonists disturbed. But that was a fairy tale; I couldn't justify letting her break the seals based on children's stories." Noah shook his head. "I regret denying her. That was what pushed her over the edge."

For the hundredth time Jacklyn found herself tearing up outside the captain's quarters. "You couldn't have let her look?"

Michiko had told her again and again that numbers were straightforward, numbers were neutral. Jacklyn had used simple, objective numbers to calculate herself out of her behavioral programs. Numbers had put her on command track. If her mother had the numbers, not to mention the support of other quartermasters across the fleet, how could her father have refused her?

"It's been a century since the fleet left. I asked her how a life-form could have lived so long onboard." Noah frowned, pausing to cough. His phlegm was the color of nutrigel. "She started talking about hibernating clutches, doors with eggs. I couldn't take any of what she said seriously."

"But she was right," Jacklyn choked out. "Now people are dead because none of us listened."

"Actually," her father said, smiling again, "there was something she got wrong."

Jacklyn was unsettled by the expression peeking through her father's unkempt hair. "What's that?"

Noah laughed. "Tegan was convinced that the creatures were monsters. She was so consumed by that fear that she died before she could see any alternative."

Jacklyn's skin crawled. She didn't see what there was to laugh about regarding her mother's death, or the ones that she had seen herself today. "What are you talking about?"

"These creatures are not our destruction," Noah insisted. "They're our salvation."

The grav system must be malfunctioning. The ventilation in Jacklyn's suit must be broken too. Otherwise the light-headedness making her feel seconds from fainting was from the revelation that something was very wrong with her father.

"I just watched those bastards tear through our crew," she breathed, dizzy with disbelief. "They slaughtered our people. What part of that sounds like *salvation* to you?"

"If you've encountered them too," Noah said excitedly, "then you know they're perfect."

Jacklyn's shameful, instinctive reaction to that was agreement. Mere flashes of the Centauri had shown that they were peak organisms: mobile, adaptable, faster and deadlier than humans by far. They had proven their ability to survive in both Terran and Centauri environments. They might even be intelligent—they had come aboard the fleet, made a home in their resources, and bided their time while they left the Proxima hellscape in search of something better.

Outrage smothered that feeling. She was going to ask

how her father could possibly say that when the implications of his statement finally hit her.

"You saw them before?" she asked, dazed.

"Almost half a year ago," Noah confirmed. "We've known for a while that the farms' output was worsening; that's why I ordered garrison rations. I went down to the silos to check our supplies and figured it out then."

Jacklyn's head ached, squeezed by the pressure of the realizations quickly crowding her mind. She put the pieces together. "You messed with the hold terminal," she said slowly.

Her father nodded. "It would've caused a panic if anyone else found out. It was bad luck that the last engagement threw all the systems out of whack and undid my hard work."

"What about Comms?" she demanded. "Are you the reason we've been struggling to contact the rest of the flotilla?"

"I scrambled our receivers a bit," he admitted. "The other ships were taking their quartermasters a little more seriously. I was avoiding a panic."

"You endangered the whole ship." Jacklyn gasped. "You let these parasites live and grow in her belly." She thought of the unnatural crunch of Vidal's body in the maintenance hatch, of the diced meat of Panio's remains, of the missing pieces of Michiko's cold corpse. She screamed, "People are dead because you lied!"

"That was the plan." Her father shrugged.

Her mouth fished open and shut for several seconds.

"You've seen the numbers, Jack. That was always your gift," he said gently. He retrieved his datapad, its surface cracked nearly to illegibility. "We're not getting six thousand people back to Earth. Not at this pace, not with what we have."

The air ripped out of Jacklyn's lungs like she had been dumped suit-less into space.

"No," she groaned. "*No.*"

"The Centauri aren't monsters," Noah said entreatingly. "They're an opportunity. One that we can't waste, not if we want to survive."

"I can't believe this." Jacklyn shook her head again and again, praying that she was in a nightmare, that she would wake up for her next shift and find her father in the ready room with a list of duties for her. She would even rather be dropped in the middle of an engagement.

"I didn't know what the precise timing would be," Noah went on, "and I didn't know how many there were. But nearly two weeks ago I saw our stats dip, and I prepared my bunk as a precaution. The Centauri are awake now, and just as hungry as I hoped."

Jacklyn felt more revulsion for her father than she had for the horrible carcasses that the creatures had made out of her crewmates and friends. "You wanted the Centauri to get rid of a few hungry mouths? You manufactured the scarcity! Those bastards ate through a silo—that food could have gotten us home."

"Not without the kind of jump that would've destroyed the ship," Noah corrected her. "We can make it if we purge about half the population. One silo is a reasonable payment for that kind of service."

"You're sick," she muttered, dazed. "How the hell would you have stopped the Centauri at just half?"

"With this." Noah hefted his datapad. "I have master

access to all parts of the ship. Once the Centauri are done, I can seal them away with a few clicks."

Jacklyn spat at his feet, too disgusted for words.

"Jack, we have two choices," he coaxed. "We can sacrifice the few for the many, or we can sacrifice them all. I chose the lesser of two evils."

"Maybe it's better that Mom and Kimmie are dead." She glared at him. "They died before they could see you like this."

The tranquil smile dropped off of her father's face. He had the nerve to look pained. "You're a survivor, Jack. I thought you of all people would understand. There are unknown enemies outside this ship with power and technology beyond our intellect. Why shouldn't we use the known enemy inside this ship to help us get home?"

Jacklyn peered as deep as she could through her father's ruined hair, trying to find some small reflection of the man who had raised her. But she saw nothing in the singularities of his eyes, just an impenetrable darkness.

"Go to hell," she said.

"Fine," Noah sighed like she had broken his heart, not the other way around. He brought his datapad up with shaky hands. "In that case, I recommend that you and your droid get in your bunk," he said, tapping at the device.

"Why?" Jacklyn asked. She realized that she hadn't yet lowered her weapon.

"Because the work isn't done," Noah declared, showing her his screen: a ship schematic, glowing a grim orange to indicate all the ship's closed doors and sealed systems. "We need to cull the herd to save it."

Jacklyn's blood went cold. Her hand twitched on her gun.

"I'm going to open the door," Noah said. He swiped a finger down the pad.

One side of the ship schematic turned green.

"No!" Jacklyn screamed, squeezing the trigger.

The plasma bolt flashed quick as lightning, arcing across the corridor and slamming into her father's chest. The shot threw him back against the wall of his bunk; the metal of the bulkhead sizzled on contact. Noah slumped to the ground with his heart cored out and replaced with a smoking hole.

The gun slid from Jacklyn's hands and hit the floor with a clatter. She tripped over her own feet and fell to her knees in front of Noah. Overhead the lights in the cabin flashed emergency red as sensors detected an interruption to the captain's vitals.

Jacklyn stared into his face. It looked unfamiliar with the muscles gone totally slack and the huge black eyes starting to droop. She had been waiting to see her father, and now that she was in front of him she was looking at a stranger.

Tears welled up and blurred her vision, pinching her nose and making her breath shudder. She started to shake so hard her teeth rattled.

Watson grabbed her tight, stopping the shaking with its unyielding grip and pulling her away.

"Jack," Watson said, sounding plaintive. "I'm sorry."

Jacklyn sobbed. This was a face that she did know. It wasn't the exact plate that Kimberly had started wearing after the engagement that ruined her real face, but it was the same model—the same shape, the same color. And it had the same effect on Jacklyn.

She dropped her head in her helmet and wept.

"Jack," Watson repeated. "I'm sorry, but you can't stay here. The Centauri are coming."

For a moment Jacklyn considered kneeling here on the captain's floor and waiting for the creatures to arrive. She had tried her best. It simply wasn't enough. Not enough to escape the engagements, not enough to rescue their stores, not enough to stop the infestation. Not enough to save her family. One minute of agony and then all her failures and shortcomings would fade away into a sea of black like the void they were sailing.

In the next moment Jacklyn snarled through her tears and lurched to her unsteady feet. She looked down at her father's body, shock and horror buzzing beneath the numbing knowledge that she had one last job to do. "I'm going to fix this," she whispered.

"We have to hurry," Watson said. "The port side lift shafts are wide open. The Centauri are climbing up."

The droid followed her as she staggered back to the corridor and scooped up her weapon. She thought fast as she led them both to the lift in question. With the shape of an idea in mind, she pointed at the lift.

"Can you crush that closed?" she asked hoarsely.

Watson looked at her quizzically but obeyed. It dug its fingers into the metal of both doors and gave a herculean squeeze, crunching and mangling them together so badly they would need to be blowtorched open.

"Good." Jacklyn sniffled. "Now listen. I'm going to go a deck below."

"What's the plan?" Watson was already doubling back down the corridor.

"You're going to stay here," she said.

The frown on Watson's face told her what the droid thought of that. "What are you going to do?"

"My dad opened up a path," Jacklyn explained, hefting her gun. "They're going to take it straight to me."

※

Jacklyn stepped onto the observation deck.

It was exactly as delta team had left it, as dark and empty as the times she had come here to think. The underfoot lighting was flickering, a good indication that she only had a little time before she wasn't alone.

She started to prepare. First she pulled out the aramid fiber line coiled in her belt, unraveling enough to secure herself to one of the observation benches. The line was designed to withstand ludicrous force and vacuum conditions—she hoped the rating was accurate, because she was about to test its capability with her life.

With her umbilical cord in place, she pulled herself to the hull, following the curve of the tall windows all the way around to the place where she normally leaned against the close press of space. There was no time even to glance at the Sun out of habit. Instead she searched the window until she found the spot she was looking for: a tiny crack in the reinforced glass, the source of the ominous noise she had heard during the grav malfunction that had sent her and Watson careening into the window.

She triple-checked her gun and gear. She had several plasma shots left—just enough for her hasty plan. She patted herself down and checked her head-up display for any holes in her suit; when she was satisfied she took a deep breath and faced the lift, waiting.

It didn't take long before the lift doors trembled with the force of something banging on them from the inside. The clanking got louder and louder until the seam between them started to widen. Through the dimness of the observation deck Jacklyn could see dark claws curl around the edges of the doors and force them apart.

The Centauri had arrived.

The darkness was so thick in the room that she could only see the creatures' massive silhouettes as they crawled out of the lift shaft. Jacklyn counted each shape as they slunk through the atrium: all four of them were here. Starlight gleamed off of their carapaces as they darted in and out of the shadows, flashes of opalescence that let Jacklyn know they were spreading out to surround her, an easy meal.

Her father's words rung in her mind. He had done the unthinkable by forfeiting lives he had sworn to protect, but a part of her could follow his logic. The Centauri were impressive organisms, exquisitely evolved. Jacklyn envied their resilience, their prowess. In another reality humans could have learned much from their survival. She wondered briefly what they could have achieved if they had lived symbiotically on Proxima b.

The deck's reserve lighting flickered out as the creatures approached. Jacklyn set her jaw and stood still, waiting.

If this didn't work, she would have sacrificed herself for nothing. That was fine—she had committed an atrocity no different from the Centauri. As long as Watson was able to inform the remaining security teams about their current position, there was still hope they could take back their ship.

One of the creatures came close enough that Jacklyn could see the scythes of its talons on the floor grates. Its huge form leaned back on its haunches, not to retreat but to pounce. Behind it, the other creatures did the same.

Jacklyn squeezed her eyes shut, waiting another heartbeat.

Then she shot her gun at the window.

The first bolt made the crack in the glass splinter across the entire panel, the seams glowing with plasma like red threads slashing across the background tapestry of the galaxy. At the edge of her vision she could see a few of the Centauri flinch back. The second shot destroyed the inner pane completely, making glass tinkle down to the deck. Jacklyn shot the rest of her remaining bolts in quick succession, trying to break the outer layer too; after several more thunderous rounds of her weapon the view of space beyond the ship fractured and then splintered into opacity.

Out of the corner of her eye she saw one of the Centauri leaping for her. She squeezed the trigger one last time.

The rest of the window shattered.

The *Calypso*'s hull breach alarms screeched to life. Even through her helmet she could hear the ear-splitting whoosh of air sucked violently out into space. Her line caught her as the suction threatened to pull her out as well, jerking her to the bench so hard that she gasped, sharp pain radiating from her back and pelvis.

A gigantic blur of black raced past her, tumbling end over end through the jagged edges of the window. It shrieked so loud that she flinched back, before the silence of space muted the noise.

She craned her neck to scan the deck with frantic eyes. The other Centauri tried to dig their claws into the grated flooring, but the evacuation of atmosphere yanked them out of the ship right after the first.

Everything went silent as the last of the air left the deck. The only thing Jacklyn could hear was her own panting and the hiss of her suit re-pressurizing. The blaring of the breach sirens faded away; she only knew they were still sounding from the emergency lights illuminating the deck in red bursts. Her feet left the ground as the ship automatically isolated the deck from the rest of the systems.

She squinted out the broken window. Faintly against the star-studded darkness she could see the outlines of the Centauri as they spun away. The creatures were off the ship.

The plan had worked.

Jacklyn felt relief shoot through her like a stimulant. Her body went limp with it; she bobbed weightlessly at the end of her line. The crew was safe. The ship was clear.

She had done it.

She needed to contact the security teams and tell them to call off the hunt. She also needed to call Watson and see if the droid could help reel her back in. There was a backlog of priorities to address now that their immediate threat was gone: releasing the crew from lockdown, resuming negotiations with the factions, ushering the repair teams back to their work. Jacklyn hoped that she could pass out before tackling that list, but there were other urgent problems as well: gathering the bodies of the officers who gave their lives, taking a census to ensure none of the rest of the crew was missing or eaten, searching all the vents and inner bulkheads and maintenance hatches onboard to make sure there were no other eggs hidden anywhere.

Right as she opened her mouth to contact the crew, she saw an iridescent shimmer out of the corner of her eye.

Her relief bled into horror.

She squeezed her eyes several times, praying she was hallucinating. But it was undeniable: the silhouettes of the creatures, dark as absorption nebulae against the background stars, were not growing smaller with distance. The oil-slick play of colors off of their exoskeletons grew brighter and brighter instead of fainter. Jacklyn's body seized with dread.

The Centauri were drifting back toward the ship.

It was impossible—the creatures shouldn't be able to maneuver in space. There was nothing for them to push off, no possible application of the third law of motion. Reeling, she looked closer—that was when she noticed the sparkles drifting off of them like stardust, tiny gas particles freezing as they escaped the creatures' carapaces.

This natural propulsion was deliberate—the Centauri were venting the air trapped inside their bodies to thrust themselves back onboard.

They were going to reach the open window of the observation deck and reenter the ship. They were going to devour Jacklyn where she was shackled to the deck. They were going to infest the ship again, and the *Calypso* was going to die just like the rest of the flotilla.

Jacklyn did the first thing she could think of.

"Jolie!" she howled through her headset. "Jolie, come in!"

Her helmet comm crackled to life instantly. "Jack," Jolie gasped through the connection. "You're alive—"

"Listen to me," Jacklyn blurted. "Space jump *now*."

Jolie sucked in a breath. "Jack, what—"

"It doesn't matter where," Jacklyn said, watching the Centauri approach faster and faster. "Pick any trajectory! You have to jump or we're all going to die."

She could see the creatures slowly running out of air, their acceleration dropping off. But they had built up enough velocity that they were going to intercept the ship again. As they drifted closer, the emergency lights rolled over their dark shells, painting them the color of human blood.

"Now!" Jacklyn screamed.

She was floating in an airless room; there were no particles surrounding her capable of transmitting vibrations or sound. When the *Calypso*'s propulsion module fired up, she couldn't hear the rumblings of its engine warming or boosters engaging.

She didn't realize they were jumping until she smashed against the wall, squashed like a bug. She felt one second of excruciating, indescribable pain, and then everything went black.

9

Jacklyn woke up in Sickbay.

Even before she opened her eyes, she knew where she was: her nostrils stung with the smell of antiseptic. The stiffness of the cot underneath her and the scratchy sheet drawn across her were familiar, as was the sluggish beep of vitals overhead.

So she was hurt. That was a pleasant surprise, since she had expected to be dead.

She felt close to it. Bone-deep weakness threatened to send her back to sleep. There was a fuzzy emptiness in her limbs, like they were detached. When she pried her eyelids apart, she had to wait a long time for her eyes to focus.

The first thing she saw was Wang sitting next to her cot, frowning at a datapad. She wondered what he was doing at her bedside; it was rare for the CMO to camp out next to patients.

She could ask him later. First she needed to know the status of the *Calypso*.

"What—" She got one word into her question before the tickle of her parched throat became a coughing fit. The pain that burst through her at that small motion made her vision go completely dark. She went rigid, lying perfectly still to keep from triggering that agony again.

"Don't do *anything*," Wang warned acidly. "I mean it, Jack. Not a single thing."

The black spots took a long time to fade from her vision. When it no longer felt like someone was twisting screws into her spine, she tried again, careful not to move this time. "How's the ship?"

Wang almost looked like he was going to withhold that information on principle. "She's fine," he finally assured her. "Don't worry about that right now."

It was impossible for Jacklyn to think about anything else. "Is the crew safe?"

"I said yes," Wang grumbled. "I also said I want you to forget about duty. You're in no shape to sit up, let alone go gallivanting around the ship."

On another day Jacklyn might've pushed back on that. Right now it ached to blink, so she simply asked, "How long have I been out?"

Wang bit his lip and looked away. Eventually he sighed. "Twenty-seven days."

Jacklyn reeled. By instinct she tried to get up and nearly blacked out again. The beeping of her vitals leaped sharply.

"What did I just say?" Wang huffed, dropping a hand on her shoulder to keep her down.

She gritted her teeth against the pain and asked, "What the hell happened?"

"We space jumped," he recounted. "On your order, I heard. But the shock absorbers couldn't suppress the g's. You were crushed."

Jacklyn remembered that split second of unbearable pressure. She was doubly surprised that she was still alive.

"I had to reconstruct a good deal of your spine," Wang continued. "You also had severe radiation poisoning from opening the ship's damn core. I used . . . unconventional methods to stabilize you." At Jacklyn's look, he elaborated, "I was able to perform cellular reconstruction using organics from the bio team's egg sample."

Jacklyn stared. ". . . The Centauri egg?" She reeled at Wang's nod. "I have Centauri organics in me?"

"Its regenerative properties outclassed anything we could synthesize," Wang explained. "Without it, you would have died."

Not in a million years could Jacklyn have imagined getting a transplant from alien tissue. Picturing the DNA of the species she had hunted and been hunted by coiling next to her own made her tremble on her cot. She fumbled for something—anything—less mind-shattering to anchor her.

"The crew?" she croaked. She tried to see if anyone else had been sent to Sickbay by the jump, but the attempt made her lose a few seconds.

"Stop that," Wang snapped. "Jolie gave the warning for the jump—most of the crew had time to grab their anti-g gear. Everyone else is already healed."

Jacklyn could hardly believe she'd been under that long. It seemed like just a few minutes ago she'd been watching the Centauri shooting toward the ship like meteoroids, soon to claw their way back in and resume their slaughter.

"The jump worked?" she marveled. She remembered all of Onyekachi's warnings about the propulsion module. The fact that it hadn't crushed them all to compost was shocking. "Where are we now?"

"About ten trillion kilometers closer to home," Wang said matter-of-factly. "Your little stunt shaved a couple centuries off our flight time."

For one addled moment Jacklyn felt a flicker of pride in

her chest. They had successfully routed an alien blight from their ship and made a space jump without tearing the *Calypso* apart. Those were wins that she desperately needed.

Unfortunately neither of those meant very much in the grand scheme of things. A few centuries off their journey still left a long time to twiddle their thumbs. Now that their stores were lightened, turned into fodder for the Centauri nest, they would never last that long, even with the boost of the jump.

"How much time left now?" she asked, wondering what level of impossibility they were dealing with.

"That's the thing," Wang said tiredly. "Now we're down to eternity."

Jacklyn stiffened. "What?"

"The jump took the last of our juice. We're just drifting now. We're not going anywhere."

Maybe a day before Jacklyn could have taken the news with grace. After months of drugged-up grief, a week of frantic secrets, and an entire day of fear and slaughter, Jacklyn's eyes flooded and her lungs shriveled up. The pressure was too much; the first sob wracked her with so much pain that she slid right back into unconsciousness.

※

When Jacklyn next awoke, her bedside was crowded. Asher was slurping a nutrigel packet and watching Jolie pace the end of the cot. She was tying anxious braids into her hair as she strode back and forth; peeking from her pocket was an abandoned embroidery project that she had clearly flubbed in her distraction. Watson, standing on Jacklyn's other side, was the first to notice that she was awake.

"Jack." It beamed.

Jolie whipped around and dove for her hand. "Hey," she said, trying to sound gentle even though it didn't suit her. "How are you doing?"

Jacklyn risked turning her head to give her a wince of a smile; the motion was only half as painful this time around. "Great."

Asher leaned into view. "Real convincing, Jack."

Jacklyn looked back and forth between them. "Who has the conn?" She grimaced at the crack of her neck in the quiet ward.

"Helm," Jolie assured her. "They have it under control."

"Easy job these days," Asher added.

That was right—the *Calypso* was just a husk now. They were wandering aimlessly, stuck at their last heading and velocity.

"How long was I out this time?" Jacklyn asked, knowing the consequences but trying to sit up anyway. The pain made her nauseous but didn't threaten to knock her back out again. That was progress.

"Another week," Wang answered from the next room over. "If you're trying to get up, Jack, I swear—"

Jacklyn obediently settled back down. "And the ship?"

"No change," Jolie sighed. "We're drifting, we're hungry, but we're alive."

Jacklyn closed her eyes. Rationally she knew that her choices had been few back on the observation deck, but that didn't stop her from feeling the crushing weight of the consequences. What was a crueler fate for her crew: quick, brutal slaughter or slow, drawn-out starvation?

"That last bit wouldn't be true without you, Jack," Asher reminded her.

Jacklyn shied away from the words. She could still see the manic look on her father's face as he tried to damn the rest of the ship to hell, the emptiness in his eyes after she shot him point-blank.

"We're going to die anyway." Jacklyn looked away. "I didn't do much of anything."

"You're so dramatic," Asher groaned.

Jolie crossed her arms. "He's right," she admonished. "Every new day that we're still alive out here is a victory— one that our forebears risked everything for. You can't minimize that."

"Damn, sorry," Jacklyn sighed. She never won when Asher and Jolie teamed up. "Thanks for holding things down."

"You're welcome," Asher said archly. "It was chaotic for a while, but now we have some semblance of normalcy again."

"Tell me?" Jacklyn requested, trying not to sound desperate.

Jolie and Asher shared a silent, deliberating look. Watson, however, had no qualms about offering the information.

"The ship was badly damaged by the jump," the droid recited. "The factions in the wards broke their strike to facilitate crisis repairs. The crew did a sweep for any remnants of the Centauri, and the bodies of those who had been killed. After the eulogies, negotiations resumed and ended favorably last week."

Jacklyn blinked. "Wow. All tied up in a bow."

"Not quite," Jolie corrected. "The fact that we lost so many officers has been hard on ship functionality. Data and Security have already announced their new heads, but we still need a purser and quartermaster."

"Most important," Asher said, treading carefully, "we still need a captain."

Jacklyn swallowed hard. She hesitated. "My father?"

"Cremated with the others," Watson reported. "His ashes are yours to do with as you will."

"The Centauri didn't get him," Jacklyn told Jolie and Asher urgently, though the plasma shot wound probably made that obvious. She needed to make sure they knew the truth. "I killed him."

"We know, Jack," Jolie said. "Watson was recording the whole time."

"Oh."

"We saw everything." Asher lobbed his nutrigel packet into a nearby recycling chute. "You're not being tried, if that's what you were angling for. Captain Albright was committing treason, which you stopped. I can't pretend to know what you're feeling right now, but no one blames you for what happened."

Jacklyn couldn't even approach that thought yet. There was so much to unpack from the last few days—or, well, the last month. For everyone else it had been weeks since the attack, but it was still fresh and oozing for her.

Asher reached down to squeeze Jacklyn's hand with the utmost care. "I need to get to the bridge. But I'm glad you're back, Jack."

"Thanks," she said, squeezing him too. He left with an offhand wave.

As soon as he was gone, Jolie came forward. Even though Watson was still in the room, she bent down and kissed Jacklyn within an inch of her life. It was very painful, but Jacklyn reciprocated as best as she could.

"You tried to sacrifice yourself." Jolie pulled back to wag her finger. "The exact opposite of what I told you to do."

"My bad," Jacklyn said sheepishly. She wanted to be suave, but she was trembling on her back on a cot she'd been occupying for a month straight and she probably needed a sonic shower. She promised shyly, "I'll make it up to you."

"Good." Jolie pulled back, satisfied. "I would have been very upset if you had died before we had a proper evening together. Now rest."

Jacklyn watched her leave, admiring the sway of her long dark hair. She wished she could get up and follow her, but she didn't want to earn Wang's wrath. She turned to Watson, standing at the edge of her cot.

"Recording, huh?" she asked, raising an eyebrow.

"I'm a data droid." Watson smiled. "It's what I do."

Sometime in the last month someone had fixed Watson's faceplate, crack and all, and replaced its chassis so that it was no longer warped from the Centauri attack. There were no breasts in sight.

"Thank you," she blurted. "We would've died a couple times over if you hadn't helped. You saved us."

Watson preened at the praise. "Thank *you*, Jack." It stepped closer to the cot and lowered its voice. "I have something to ask you, when you recover."

Jacklyn tried to think of what Watson wanted to discuss— only Otto came to mind. The thought of him made the vitals above her cot pick up. She wished he weren't dead just so she could beat his ass. "You do realize I'm going to be wondering what you mean for the entire time that I'm stuck here."

"You'll just have to heal faster," Watson said placidly.

"Was that teasing?" Jacklyn's eyes went wide.

"I've been studying."

Jacklyn groaned, dropping her head back down to her pillow.

She was relieved that the ship had gone on smoothly without her, but the things yet undone nagged at her. Even though she hadn't moved since she woke up, she felt very weak after all that talking.

"Rest, Jack," Watson said, but Jacklyn was already drifting off.

✳

It took another week for Jacklyn to escape bed rest. When she recovered the strength to sit up, Wang handed her over to the ship's physical therapist. She had to wear a special uniform with a built-in brace while she relearned how to walk. By then she was accepting Watson's offers to assist her prescribed exercises just to break the monotony of Sickbay. She deliberately didn't think about how quickly her recovery was progressing or why.

Jolie stayed with her in her bunk after her release, ostensibly to monitor her progress. It wasn't all honeymoon— Jolie spent as much time holding Jacklyn's braids back as she vomited and cried from nightmares as she did making Jacklyn cry out for much more enjoyable reasons.

Jacklyn had to go back to Sickbay to intensify her meds.

She didn't protest the addition of a regular therapist, not when the faces of Panio, Michiko, and her father still haunted her.

She resumed her patrols; she couldn't do full rounds anymore, but it was more of a compulsion than ever. Every time she passed a deck and heard the familiar sounds of the *Calypso*'s heartbeat instead of banging in the walls, she breathed easier.

At the first briefing she attended after waking up, she was asked to be acting captain. Her immediate refusal was followed by an hour of debate that ultimately convinced her it was the best choice for the ship; she had taken over so many of her father's duties in the end that it was simpler to have her continue in that capacity.

Not long after she was back on duty, the bio researchers called her to their reconstructed lab. They had spent the month wringing every bit of knowledge they could out of the Centauri egg, monitoring its growth and development. They had concluded that the life cycle of the creatures was long; their cells possessed some kind of endospores which allowed them to lie dormant and remain viable for long periods. That was how they had lasted in the ship's stores and walls. Now that the mature Centauri were off the ship, however, the egg was deteriorating. They estimated that it and any other un-nursed eggs would die completely in another month. So ended humankind's first and possibly last astrobiological breakthrough.

After a few days back on light duty, Jacklyn decided she was well enough to take care of the matter that had been bugging her since she woke up.

She found Watson in Data, standing in Otto's old office. It had been rigorously cleaned, so pristine that no one except she and the droid would know what had happened there.

A new head of Data had already been appointed, but they wouldn't move in until new terminals were installed. The office was completely bare around the two of them.

"Jack," Watson greeted her, pleased to be found. "How are you feeling today?"

"Like I'm ready to hear whatever secret you've been keeping," Jacklyn grumbled.

"Are you fully recovered?" the droid asked suspiciously.

"Does it matter?" Jacklyn huffed. "Spare me the suspense."

Watson had been supervising her recovery closely, making sure Jacklyn followed her therapy plan even when she wanted to say to hell with it and jump back in the saddle. For the past day, however, the droid had been nowhere to be found.

"What was your question?" Jacklyn asked.

Watson surprised her by pulling out a small input chip. "I wanted to talk about this."

Jacklyn remembered pocketing the chip she'd found next to Otto's body, the one that came with the note. "You want to plug that in," she realized.

"I've thought about it," Watson admitted. "The doctor said the contents of this chip could get us home. We have nothing to lose by trying now."

"He said a lot of things," Jacklyn growled. She didn't want Otto influencing the droid from beyond the grave. "You don't need to do that. We're going to figure something else out."

"What if he already did?" Watson asked.

"I don't trust anything he wanted to do to you," Jacklyn said frankly.

"I want to save the ship like you, Jack."

Jacklyn hesitated. She had spent all of her recent waking hours trying to figure out what to do about the *Calypso*'s fate. Every engineer or techie who wasn't on repairs was working with a much-revived Onyekachi on the propulsion module, but they'd had no luck yet. Jacklyn had gotten them into this mess and felt obligated to get them out, but she didn't have any ideas on how to do so. Until now.

Right as she opened her mouth to speak, she felt the ship shudder with a distant vibration. A second later the whole thing rocked.

Jacklyn tipped over. Even with the brace she wasn't strong enough to keep her feet on the rolling deck. Watson lunged, catching her before she could brain herself on the floor.

"God*damn it*," Jacklyn hissed.

The grav system flickered as the ship bucked again. Watson helped Jacklyn turn on her magnetic soles and pushed her back upright. She tried to run out of Data and back to the lift, but she only got as far as the atrium before her fledgling strength ran out. Wordlessly, Watson picked her up and carried her the rest of the way to the bridge.

Asher was in command, focusing on the viewfinder with sweat beading on his brow. "You're not supposed to be here," he said without looking, analyzing the trajectories crisscrossing the screen.

"Well, I am." Jacklyn leaned heavily on Watson as she hobbled to the captain's chair. Asher got to his feet and switched places. "Give me an update."

Another engagement, as she thought. The helmsman steered them on the remnants of their thruster power according to the updates on the viewfinder. Comms monitored internal damage reports as injuries mounted, nowhere near as severe as the last engagement.

Jacklyn didn't let down her guard. She frowned at the options, none of which were particularly compelling. "Asher, the stats?"

"Nothing above a thirty-nine percent," he said, scanning his datapad.

Jacklyn scowled. "Where the hell are we supposed to go?"

"Jack," Watson interjected. "I think I know."

Jacklyn spun the chair around and froze.

Watson's eyes were the wrong color again, though not like before. They weren't the sickly yellow from the Centauri attack, but an eerie shade of purple that Jacklyn had never encountered—the unseeable purple of a supergiant star, or the cosmic purple of a celestial event. The droid pulled aside the top of its uniform to show Jacklyn where it had inserted Otto's data chip without saying anything.

Jacklyn's stomach dropped.

"The doctor did it," Watson marveled. "I can hear *them*."

Gooseflesh sped across Jacklyn's limbs, but before she could tell Watson to yank out the chip, the droid continued dreamily, "Let me ask—"

When Watson opened its mouth, the whale song came out, clearer than ever; below the long notes Jacklyn could hear a kind of lilting melody, and under that little staccato beats that reminded her once again of a language she couldn't decipher. It sounded like the seismic breath of stars, like the roar of a magnetic bow shock, like the gossipy vibrations of interstellar plasma.

It sounded like a conversation between gods.

The whale song cut out as Watson's face broke into a grin. "It's the way."

It held its hand out toward the viewfinder—before the bridge crew's eyes another trajectory blinked onto the screen, the same otherworldly purple as the droid's wide eyes. It looked like nothing the simulations had produced before, an arrow-straight shot toward one of the stars in their view with no concern for the starbursts plotted in its path.

Jacklyn looked back and forth between the screen and the droid. She didn't know what the hell Otto's chip had awoken in it, if she could trust what Watson was saying.

Watson turned its glowing eyes on her. "The way home," it clarified.

Smoke began to pour from underneath its uniform, and an ominous rattling started up in its chassis like a terrible cough. Whatever the chip was doing was hurting it; Jacklyn felt panic rise in her own chest, climbing her throat until it was pushing out of her mouth.

"Take the course," she blurted.

"Jack—" Asher wavered, but the ship was already maneuvering.

As soon as they slid onto the trajectory, the shaking of the ship completely ceased. The sudden absence of blaring klaxons left the bridge in eerie silence. A chill shuddered down Jacklyn's spine as she glanced around: the screens on every console had blanked out to that same odd color. The officers at each station fiddled with their controls, but the takeover spread until the whole bridge glowed purple.

Jacklyn had a moment to wonder if she had made the wrong call, before the ship lurched forward through space.

The stars in the viewfinder stretched into long, blinding

tails as they jumped. Jacklyn waited for the g's to crush her again, but the pressure never came. This was nothing like a space jump from their own engines—this one was smooth and controlled. It was a jump utterly beyond their capabilities.

Someone else was moving the ship.

The jump only lasted a few seconds, just long enough for the bridge crew to cry out. It ended with a bone-rattling jolt as the ship was dumped off the cosmic fast lane, a concussive jerk so powerful that it launched everyone from their seats.

Jacklyn was flung out of the captain's chair. She hit the floor hard, head bouncing as she landed in a heap. She lay there, dazed, and heard the groans and gasps of other officers around the deck doing the same.

When her head stopped spinning, Jacklyn clawed her way back into the captain's chair. From there she could see the whole bridge. Asher was sprawled next to the chair, his temple bright red where he'd hit his face on the way down. Other officers were still shaking off the shock as they stumbled back to their stations. Jacklyn barely had time to celebrate the fact that no one was dead before her eyes fell on Watson.

The droid was laid out on the ground. Its face was still fixed in a bright smile, but its chassis was blown open, smoking from the overload of its components. The lattice inside had burst.

Jacklyn stumbled over to the droid. "Watson, wake up."

Nothing happened. No processes whirred on; there was no response to the voice command. Jacklyn grabbed Otto's chip and flung it away.

"Hey," she said louder. She took the droid's shoulders and shook it to the best of her ability. It barely budged, but a little blue did come back to its eyes.

"Jack," it whispered, voice reduced to static. "The tasks worked. *They* heard me too."

"You're hurt," Jacklyn said helplessly. Too late, she understood who *they* were: the ones to whom they had been trying to wave a white flag this whole time. "Why did you do that?"

"I asked for parley, like the doctor said. I told them we weren't supposed to be there." Watson gave a pixelated cough. "They moved us out of the way."

"Sit tight," Jacklyn interrupted, cupping that familiar face. She started to shake as the vision before her overlapped with her memories. "I'll get you fixed up soon."

"See you planetside, Jack," Watson said, right before going dark.

Jacklyn sat back, feeling a space yawning open in her chest, the one she thought she had closed after burning her mother's body, after burning her sister's. Her eyes blurred; she tore her gaze away from the droid before she sobbed.

It fell on the viewfinder instead. Without the readings, schematics, or trajectory overlays, the viewfinder just projected the *Calypso*'s clear view of the void. Even through tears, on the screen Jacklyn could see a star. She gasped wetly.

It was larger and closer than any star she had ever observed before, so bright in comparison that she had to glance away, blinking spots out of her stinging eyes. Its golden glow spilled across the bridge like ambrosia, warmer than the cold starlight she had known all her life.

She scrambled to the nearest console, fumbling with the controls to polarize the screen. When the worst of the brightness was filtered, she took another look out into the system where they had been delivered.

She could see the enormous limb of some huge planet, so big that it took up the whole corner of the screen. It was a Jovian, banded with turbulent layers of red, browns, and golds. The hurricanes raging in its chromophoric clouds formed whorls and eddies in the colors. At the bottom of the limb swirled an almost-spent storm, cannibalized at the edges by tinier, more voracious cyclones.

Jacklyn put a hand over her mouth. She knew that red spot.

She had seen pictures of this planet her whole childhood, along with the other seven in this system. She pressed herself against the viewfinder, scanning the little pinpricks of light spattered across the polarized view. She was looking for one in particular; she squinted until it hurt, until she found it.

It was just as they said: a pale blue dot.

Behind her, the bridge erupted with cries of the same wonder choking her throat. She didn't look away from the Sun, no longer a stitch but a whole brooch pinned to the black fabric of the void. All her life she had stared at this tiny thread—now it was the center of a new tapestry, one both unfamiliar and known. She fixed her eyes on the planet sitting like a tiny jewel in the embroidered starscape on the screen.

It was home.

ACKNOWLEDGMENTS

I finished this novella in a little under a month, a feat that would not have been possible without the support of my wonderful family and friends. Its publication would not have been possible without the tirelessness of the fantastic teams who facilitated this debut.

Sara Lafferty, thank you for being a part of all my milestones for the last decade and a half. I appreciate your kind read-through of this rush job and your reassurance that I had a chance. Thank you for being my best friend.

Melissa, thank you for reading my first draft at ass o'clock in the morning and offering me your spot-on commentary. Thank you for always believing in my work and letting me devour yours.

Hannah Fergesen, thank you for seeing my potential and taking care of me to the end. Chelsea Hensley, thank you for getting excited about me and guiding me the rest of the way. Thank you to kt literary for being a community I'm so thrilled to be a part of.

Kristin Temple, thank you for your incredible insight and guidance in the polishing of this novella and in the publishing process as a whole. Melanie Sanders, thank you for your eagle-eyed attention and very necessary fine-tuning. Chris McGrath, Russell Trakhtenberg, and Greg Collins, thank you for the incredible face you've given to the novella. Sara-ciea Fennell and Jordan Hanley, thank you for giving this book the best possible introduction to the world. To the entire Nightfire team, thank you for your belief, your time and effort, and your expertise. None of this would have been possible otherwise.

Chloe Gong, David Wellington, S. A. Barnes, Gemma Files, Ada Hoffmann, Livia Llewellyn, and Ally Wilkes, thank you for the time and kindness you invested in reading *Scourge* and writing such generous words about it.

Trula Howe, Mark Brown, and Toni Brown, thank you for being possibly more excited about each step of this journey than I was. Thank you for celebrating everything with me, for being my biggest cheerleaders, and for lifting me up to who and where I am today.

David Park, thank you for telling me to do this, for not complaining about me coming to bed at two in the morning every night for a month, and for believing wholeheartedly in me, even though you never actually finished reading the draft. I love you to the moon and back.

ABOUT THE AUTHOR

Meghan Kelly of NY Headshots

NESS BROWN is a speculative fiction author by day and astrophysicist by night. They are a proud New Mexican living in New York City (and missing green chile) with their husband and two cats, Faust and Mephi. They are currently studying graduate astrophysics after several years of teaching astronomy and encouraging students to wonder about worlds beyond our own. *The Scourge Between Stars* is their debut.